WITHDRAWN
www.hants.gov.uk/library
Hampshire
County Council
Love
YOUR LIBRARY
Tel: 0300 555 1387
D0336467

Jane Austen's

PERSUASION

AWESOMELY AUSTEN

Illustrated by Églantine Ceulemans

Pride and Prejudice – Katherine Woodfine

Emma – Katy Birchall

Persuasion – Narinder Dhami

Sense and Sensibility – Joanna Nadin

Mansfield Park – Ayisha Malik

Northanger Abbey – Steven Butler

Jane Austen's
Persuasion

Retold by Narinder Dhami
Illustrated by Églantine Ceulemans

Hodder

First published in Great Britain in 2019 by Hodder and Stoughton

1 3 5 7 9 10 8 6 4 2

All characters and events in this publication, other than those clearly in the public domain, are fictitious and any resemblance to real persons, living or dead, is purely coincidental.

A CIP catalogue record for this book
is available from the British Library.

ISBN 978 1 444 95063 2

Typeset in Bembo by Hewer Text UK Ltd, Edinburgh
Printed and bound in Great Britain by Clays Ltd, Elcograf S.p.A

The paper and board used in this book
are made from wood from responsible sources.

Hodder Children's Books
An imprint of
Hachette Children's Group
Part of Hodder and Stoughton
Carmelite House
50 Victoria Embankment
London EC4Y 0DZ

An Hachette UK Company
www.hachette.co.uk

www.hachettechildrens.co.uk

Persuasion, by Jane Austen, was first published in 1817.

This was the Regency era – a time when English society was sharply divided by wealth and women were expected to marry young.

The heroine of this story, Anne, might have some things in common with modern readers, but she lived in a very different world.

You can find out more about Jane Austen and what England was like in 1817 at the back of this book!

MAIN CHARACTERS

SIR WALTER ELLIOT

Vain, wealthy and reckless with money, Sir Walter must rent out his home – Kellynch Hall – to pay his debts. Father of three grown-up daughters.

MISS ELIZABETH ELLIOT

The eldest sister, and Sir Walter Elliot's favourite daughter.

MISS ANNE ELLIOT

Our heroine! Kind and generous, she has never got over her first love, Captain Wentworth.

MRS MARY MUSGROVE

The youngest Elliot sister, she is married to Mr Charles Musrove.

MR CHARLES MUSGROVE

Charles and Mary Musgrove live at Uppercross, on the grounds of his parents' grand house.

LITTLE CHARLES AND LITTLE WALTER MUSGROVE

Children of Mary and Charles.

MR AND MRS MUSGROVE

Parents of a large family, including three grown-up children (Henrietta, Louisa and Charles).

MISS HENRIETTA MUSGROVE

Younger sister of Charles, lives with her parents. Is very close with Mr Charles Hayter.

MISS LOUISA MUSGROVE

Younger sister of Charles and Henrietta, lives with her parents. Lively and determined.

LADY RUSSELL

A very close friend of the Elliot family, Miss Anne Elliot has turned to Lady Russell for advice ever since her mother died. She lives close to Kellynch Hall.

MR WILLIAM ELLIOT

A distant relative of Sir Walter Elliot and his only male heir, so will inherit Kellynch Hall one day.

MR CHARLES HAYTER

A relative of the Musgroves, Charles is a gentleman farmer.

CAPTAIN FREDERICK WENTWORTH

A sailor who was once engaged to Miss Anne Elliot.

CAPTAIN AND MRS HARVILLE

Close friends of Captain Wentworth. They live in Lyme.

CAPTAIN BENWICK

A close friend of Captain Wentworth, living with Captain and Mrs Harville while he grieves the death of his fiancée – Captain Harville's sister.

ADMIRAL AND MRS CROFT

Recently returned from sea, Admiral Croft rents Kellynch Hall from Sir Walter Elliot.

MRS CLAY

A widow, and the daughter of the Elliot family's solicitor – Mr Shepherd. She is great friends with Miss Elizabeth Elliot.

CHAPTER ONE

'Elizabeth, my dear, we *must* economise!' Sir Walter Elliot said gloomily to his favourite daughter. He waved a hand at the pile of bills on his desk. 'I have spent nothing but what the owner of Kellynch Hall and a man of my social standing *should* spend – and yet we are in debt.'

'But, Papa, we have already cut our expenses to the bone!' Elizabeth protested sulkily. She was a tall, good-looking young woman who enjoyed spending money as much as her father did. 'Didn't we agree to stop giving to some of our charities? Didn't we decide not to buy new furniture for the drawing room? *And*' – Elizabeth glanced at her younger sister, Anne, who was sitting reading quietly beside the roaring fire – 'we also saved money by not bringing Anne a present when you and I returned from our trip to London. *Surely* all this means we can now pay our debts?'

Anne did not look up from her book, although she couldn't help overhearing the conversation. Their home, Kellynch Hall, was a large, grand house, surrounded by many acres of land, all owned by Sir Walter. The land brought the Elliot family a good income, but Anne had realised that her father had been over-spending for a very long time. When his wife, Lady Elliot, was alive, she'd managed the family's money and prevented Sir Walter from frittering it away. But Lady Elliot had become ill and died some years ago. Anne sighed gently, a sigh heard by no one else in the room.

If only Mama was still here, she thought, her dark eyes filled with sadness. *How different things would be!*

'Papa, perhaps it's time to think about selling

off some of the Kellynch land,' Elizabeth began, but Sir Walter immediately shook his head.

'Never!' he declared dramatically, glancing at himself in the mirror to admire how handsome he looked as he spoke. 'The Kellynch estate shall be passed on whole and entire to the man who succeeds me.' Then he frowned and added, 'Even though Mr William Elliot certainly does *not* deserve it!'

Anne knew that William Elliot, a distant relative of the family, was very definitely not a favourite of her father's. Sir Walter and Elizabeth had met the young man who would inherit Kellynch Hall in London, several years ago. Anne suspected that her father had secretly hoped William Elliot would propose marriage to Elizabeth, and then they could keep Kellynch Hall within their immediate family. William Elliot had been polite and friendly, but then he'd gone off and married someone else, a very rich woman of whom Sir Walter did not approve.

Added to this, William Elliot had then made some extremely rude and disrespectful remarks about Sir Walter and his eldest daughter. These remarks had been reported back to them, and a furious Sir Walter and Elizabeth had never seen or spoken to William Elliot since.

But now we have heard that Mr Elliot's wife has sadly died, perhaps Elizabeth is hoping she may have another chance to marry him, Anne thought. She had no idea how Elizabeth felt about the matter, though. There was little affection, understanding and friendship between the two of them, which upset Anne. She had a closer relationship with their youngest sister, Mary, who was married and lived not far from Kellynch, although Mary, too, could be difficult at times.

'How unfortunate and ill-used we are, Papa!' Elizabeth complained bitterly. 'Our family is so important and so well-respected. How *can* we be in this terrible situation?'

Anne remained silent. She was ashamed of having so much family debt and longed to offer some suggestions as to how they could pay back the money they owed. But she knew her father and Elizabeth wouldn't listen to anything she said. To them, she was 'only Anne' – quiet, uninteresting and of no importance whatsoever.

'My dear Elizabeth, do not despair,' Sir Walter replied absently. He was only half-listening because he was once again admiring himself in the mirror. The cut of his orange silk waistcoat was *particularly* good, he thought with pleasure, although it had cost a great deal of money. But a man like himself had to be smartly dressed at all times. It was expected. And Elizabeth looked very well, too, in her expensive lace gown. They were a handsome pair, Sir Walter thought smugly, unlike the people around them. There was Anne, so small and thin and pale. And last time he'd seen his youngest daughter, Mary, her complexion had looked so rough and red!

'I have an idea that will no doubt ease our worries,' Sir Walter went on. 'I shall seek advice from our two closest friends, Lady Russell and Mr Shepherd. I'm sure they will have a solution to offer us.'

'Very well, Papa,' Elizabeth replied, brightening up a little. 'But I warn you, I can't be expected to give up my horses, my carriage, my maids, my new dresses or our trips to London.'

'Of course not, my dear!' Sir Walter exclaimed, shocked. 'There's no need to go *that* far.'

Anne wasn't so sure. It appeared that her father and sister expected to be told how they could save money without cutting out any of their luxuries. Mr Shepherd, who was the Elliot family lawyer, usually agreed with everything Sir Walter said, so Anne had no hopes of any support from *him*. But Lady Russell was different. She had been a close friend of Lady Elliot, Anne's mother, and was a very sensible, straightforward woman whom Anne loved dearly. Perhaps Lady Russell would be able to talk Sir Walter and Elizabeth into making some big changes. Anne certainly hoped so.

'Lady Russell will be glad to help, I'm sure.' Anne spoke up at last in her soft, gentle voice. 'It's a very good idea to ask her, Papa.'

'Yes,' Sir Walter agreed. 'However, I do wish Lady Russell didn't have *quite* so many wrinkles, especially around her eyes. I felt quite upset when I noticed how bad they were when she visited last week. And she and I are of the same age! Incredible!'

'Lady Russell certainly does not look as youthful and handsome as *you* do, Papa,' Elizabeth replied, smiling.

'True,' Sir Walter agreed with high good humour. 'You and I are blooming, my dear, even if everyone around us is ageing rapidly!'

Looking very pleased with themselves, Sir Walter and Elizabeth left the room together.

Meanwhile, Anne closed her book and thought over what she'd just heard. She was pleased that Lady Russell was to be involved, but she felt very anxious, too.

Would her father and sister agree to any economies? And if they did not, then what on earth would become of them all? Anne decided that she must visit Lady Russell straight away and talk things through with her, as she so often did.

CHAPTER TWO

'My dear Anne, your advice has been so very useful!' Lady Russell said affectionately as she studied the figures she had been scribbling down on paper. She was extremely fond of Anne, and wished that Sir Walter and Elizabeth would realise how clever and lovely Anne was. 'If only we can persuade your father to accept these cuts, then he should be clear of all debt in seven years' time.'

'Yes,' Anne replied, but a little doubtfully. She had hoped the debt could be paid back more quickly. However, Lady Russell believed that Sir Walter should be allowed to live like the gentleman and landowner he was, and so she'd changed and toned down some of Anne's suggestions. But secretly Anne could hardly believe that her Father and Elizabeth would accept *any* change in their style of living, however small.

Anne was proved right. When she and Lady Russell met with Sir Walter, Elizabeth and Mr Shepherd in the drawing room later that day, there was uproar when Lady Russell explained her seven-year plan for paying back the debts.

'What!' Sir Walter exclaimed, his face turning purple with rage. 'You are not *serious*, Lady Russell?'

'No trips to London, no maids, half the horses to be sold?' Elizabeth was at her most cold and haughty as she glared at Lady Russell. 'Only *two* new gowns a year? Impossible!'

'Impossible indeed!' Sir Walter agreed furiously. 'I would rather quit Kellynch Hall at once than stay here on such disgraceful terms!'

'Ah, now that might be the very thing, Sir Walter,' Mr Shepherd said, quickly leaping into the conversation when he saw which way the wind was blowing. He was a cautious, long-faced lawyer who knew Sir Walter had to be treated with care. 'You have so many expenses here at Kellynch Hall. If you and your family moved out, you could live very well on less money somewhere else.'

Anne felt a thrill of horror run through her. Leave Kellynch Hall, the beautiful place she'd called home all her life? The home where she had so many happy memories of her mother? Surely her father would not willingly to agree to Mr Shepherd's suggestion! But to Anne's despair, she saw her father and Elizabeth exchange a swift glance of approval.

'That seems like a sensible idea, Shepherd,' Sir Walter said thoughtfully. 'We could find a splendid house to rent in London, could we not?'

'Certainly,' Mr Shepherd agreed easily, 'although you might find that the elegant city of Bath suits you and your daughters better.'

'Indeed, I think Mr Shepherd is right,' Lady Russell said hastily. Anne guessed both Lady Russell and Mr Shepherd knew that Sir Walter could not be trusted in London where everything was so expensive! 'Consider the advantages of Bath, my dear Sir Walter. It is only fifty miles from Kellynch, and a man of your standing can live there very well and much more cheaply than in London. And as you know, I spend part of every year in Bath myself.'

Anne's low spirits fell even further. For several reasons, she disliked Bath. While Sir Walter and Elizabeth were discussing their proposed move with Mr Shepherd, Anne turned to Lady Russell.

'Perhaps Papa might be happier to stay nearer Kellynch,' Anne suggested quietly to her friend. 'We could find a smaller house here in the village.'

Lady Russell shook her head at once. 'Oh no, my dear,' she said. 'Consider how your father would feel. All his neighbours would know why he'd had to leave Kellynch Hall. He would be so very embarrassed.'

Anne sighed. She saw the force of Lady Russell's argument, but still, she couldn't look forward to going to Bath.

'I understand why you do not like Bath.' Lady Russell patted Anne's hand gently. 'You were sent to school there after your dear mother died, so your memories of the city are not happy ones. And you were not in good spirits on your second visit there with me, some seven or eight years ago, I recall.'

Anne stared down at the floor. She remembered exactly *why* she had not been in good spirits on that second visit to Bath. The memory of it still caused her pain.

'Then to Bath we shall go!' Sir Walter announced with a smile. 'We must start searching for a suitable house, Elizabeth.'

'Certainly,' Elizabeth agreed eagerly. 'We shall rent a stylish and elegant property, shall we not, Papa?'

'And in the meantime, I will advertise for someone to rent Kellynch Hall,' Mr Shepherd added.

Sir Walter drew himself up to his full height and fixed his lawyer with a furious glare. '*Advertise?*' he thundered. 'I forbid you to advertise my home and estate for rent as if I was a common landlord! I forbid it, Shepherd. Do you hear me, man?'

'Very well, Sir Walter,' Mr Shepherd muttered.

Anne wondered how anyone looking for a country house to rent would know that Kellynch Hall was available if Sir Walter refused to allow it to be advertised. So she clung to this as her only hope of remaining in her beloved home for a little while longer. But unluckily for Anne, it was only a few days later that Mr Shepherd arrived with some important news. He brought with him his daughter, Mrs Clay, who was a close friend of Elizabeth's.

Neither Anne nor Lady Russell was fond of Mrs Clay. Lady Russell was annoyed that Elizabeth chose to be friends with the lawyer's daughter, instead of spending more time with her sister Anne. Mrs Clay had returned to live with her father after her husband died, and Anne strongly suspected that she was on the lookout for a new husband.

'My dear Penelope!' Elizabeth exclaimed warmly as Mrs Clay and Mr Shepherd were shown into the drawing room. 'How wonderful to see you. Come and sit beside me.'

Anne noticed Mrs Clay flash a sweet smile at Sir Walter as she went to join Elizabeth.

'I have, of course, followed your advice, Sir Walter,' Mr Shepherd began pompously. 'I have not advertised that Kellynch Hall is for rent. And yet, because you are such an important person, Sir Walter, with so many eyes upon you, it seems possible that someone may have heard a rumour and spread it around.'

Sir Walter looked torn between the embarrassment of it being publicly known that he was short of money, and the pleasure of being the subject of gossip.

'There are many rich navy officers who are coming home after the end of the war,' Mr Shepherd continued, 'and I think there could be no better tenant for Kellynch Hall than one of our brave sailors.'

'A sailor!' Sir Walter exclaimed in a very displeased tone. 'If a sailor came to live at Kellynch Hall, he would consider himself a very lucky man! I am not convinced I would allow a soldier or a sailor to rent my house.'

'Surely the navy, who have done so much to keep our country safe, deserve their home comforts even more than the rest of us?' Anne pointed out, finding the courage from somewhere to speak up.

'The navy has its uses, certainly,' Sir Walter replied coldly. 'But I would be sorry to see any friend of mine become a sailor! The seafaring life is a hard one, and it changes their appearance quite dreadfully. Why, I was introduced to an Admiral Baldwin some years back, and from his rough, weather-beaten face, I thought he was around sixty years of age. I later discovered he was but forty years old! I was quite shocked. It's a pity sailors are not knocked on the head before they reach Admiral Baldwin's age!'

'Oh, Sir Walter, do have mercy on these poor

sailors!' Mrs Clay cried. 'Not all men are lucky enough to be a high-born gentleman, and blessed with great good looks, a charming appearance and perfect health.' Sir Walter beamed at Mrs Clay, who smiled brightly back at him. Anne saw it all.

'I have had an enquiry from an Admiral Croft about renting Kellynch Hall,' Mr Shepherd announced cautiously. 'He's a little weather-beaten for sure, my dear Sir Walter, but very eager and friendly, and ready to pay whatever rent we ask. He is also married to an extremely well-spoken, sensible lady, who has travelled the world with him. In fact, Mrs Croft has connections with the village of Monkford, not far from here. Her brothers lived there for a while.' Mr Shepherd frowned. 'I cannot recall their names, however. Penelope, do you remember what Mrs Croft told us about her brothers?'

Mrs Clay was deep in private conversation with Elizabeth on the other side of the room so did not hear. But Anne did.

Anne made her excuses and escaped from the drawing room. She knew exactly whom *one* of Mrs Croft's brothers was, and she felt quite overwhelmed by her memories of him. As she wandered out into the garden, glad to feel the cool air on her flushed cheeks, she murmured to herself, 'A few months more, and *he*, perhaps, may be walking here.'

CHAPTER THREE

'*He*' was Captain Frederick Wentworth. He had been living with his brother in Monkford when he met Anne for the first time. At nineteen, Frederick and Anne had fallen deeply in love. Frederick Wentworth was a sailor. He was handsome, energetic and confident, and full of plans for the future. He intended to marry the pretty, gentle, sensitive girl who had so quickly won his heart, and then make his fortune so they could spend the rest of their lives together in comfort. Anne, glowing with happiness, had accepted his proposal of marriage immediately.

But the young couple's dreams were soon shattered into pieces. When Sir Walter was asked to agree to the marriage, he was cold and disapproving. 'Who is this Frederick Wentworth?' he'd asked scornfully. 'A nobody with little money, from an unimportant family! And he dares to ask for the hand of *my* daughter in marriage? He must have a very good opinion of himself.'

To Anne's dismay, Lady Russell, too, had been against the marriage. Captain Wentworth had not pleased her. He was brilliant, but he was headstrong, and he might *not* make his fortune. Then what would happen? Lady Russell could not bear to see Anne throw herself away, at the young age of nineteen, on such a man. So she had set out to persuade Anne to break off the engagement.

'My dear, you must see that it would be foolish to enter into such a marriage,' Lady Russell had told Anne earnestly. 'This young man has no land or property, and your father has already said that he does not approve of him. Sir Walter will not settle any money on you if you marry Captain

Wentworth. It would be madness to marry and try to live on a sailor's low wages! This engagement is a disaster, for Frederick Wentworth as well as for yourself. You *must* change your mind, Anne.'

Anne was torn. Young though she was, she felt she could have stood up to her father, even though Elizabeth offered her no sisterly support. But she had found it very difficult to ignore Lady Russell's advice. She was the closest Anne had to a mother, and her dearest friend. No, she could not disregard what Lady Russell was saying. She only had Anne's best interest at heart.

Her heart breaking, Anne had decided it would be best to call off the engagement. She couldn't have done it unless she felt that it was right for Frederick, as well as herself. But Captain Wentworth did not see it that way. A very painful meeting between the two of them had taken place when she told him she had changed her mind.

'Perhaps it is for the best, after all,' Frederick

had said coldly, his face white and unhappy. 'I do not want a wife who is so easily persuaded to do what she knows very well is wrong.'

He had left Monkford the same day, and Anne had not seen him since. The memory of that last conversation still had the power to distress her, though, even now. Anne had never met anyone else to replace Captain Wentworth. She had not much chance to do so as she spent most of her time at home, except for one miserable trip to Bath with Lady Russell shortly after their break-up.

There had been a slight possibility of marriage when a local gentleman, Charles Musgrove, had come calling on Anne. But Anne had not encouraged his interest, and finally he had asked her younger sister, Mary, to marry him instead. Mary had gladly accepted. Lady Russell was disappointed when Anne turned down Charles Musgrove. But she still didn't regret her advice to Anne to break off her engagement.

However, Anne *did* regret listening to Lady Russell all those years ago. She did not blame her friend at all, but she wished that she herself had shown a little more courage, a little more confidence. Captain Wentworth had made his fortune, as he'd said he would, and he was now a rich man, richer than Sir Walter. But Anne had never heard any report of him being married.

And now Captain Wentworth's older sister, Mrs Croft, and her husband the Admiral were eager to rent Kellynch Hall! Anne hardly knew how she felt about it. She would have to meet with the Crofts at some point, and she felt rather uncomfortable at the thought. However, Anne was quite confident that no one but herself, Captain Wentworth, Sir Walter, Elizabeth and Lady Russell knew of their short engagement. Mrs Croft had been abroad with her husband at the time, and Mary, Anne's other sister, had been away at school.

On the morning Admiral and Mrs Croft were due to visit Kellynch Hall, Anne walked over to visit Lady Russell, as she did almost every day. She wanted to keep out of their way, and only returned when she was sure they would be gone.

By the time she got home, she found that the

whole business had been settled. The Crofts were to rent Kellynch Hall, and the Elliots were to move to Bath as soon as possible. Elizabeth and Mrs Croft had been very pleased with each other. Mr Shepherd had cunningly told Sir Walter beforehand that the Crofts had heard what a polite, charming and well-bred man he was, and so Sir Walter had been on his best behaviour.

'I believe Admiral Croft to be the best-looking sailor I have ever seen!' Sir Walter announced graciously to his daughters. 'And if my own manservant might make a few changes to the Admiral's hair, I would not mind being seen anywhere with him.'

'And you are to leave for Bath so soon?' exclaimed Lady Russell. Her friend had not expected matters to be settled so quickly, Anne thought. Neither had she. It was a shock, and not a pleasant one, either.

'Of course, Lady Russell,' Elizabeth replied

impatiently. 'We must find a suitable house immediately. Mr Shepherd, do you have the list of houses for rent in Bath?'

Lady Russell frowned as Sir Walter, Elizabeth and Mr Shepherd began looking over the list. 'I am sorry you are to be rushed away like this, Anne,' she murmured. 'I had hoped you would all remain at Kellynch Hall some while longer. I would love for you to stay with me as my guest until Christmas, at least, and then I could have taken you to Bath, as I'm going there myself. However, I am leaving to stay with friends in Scotland shortly, and so I won't be at home.'

Anne sighed. She, too, would have enjoyed staying with Lady Russell for a while before finally leaving for Bath. There was little point in her going now, as she knew she would not be allowed any say in the house they were to rent. Her opinion was of no importance, even though she would be living there, too. She would just have to make her mind up to go to Bath with a willing heart. It was her only option.

However, Mary, Anne's younger sister, had other ideas. The next day she sent a message begging Anne to come and stay with her, her husband Charles and their two young children at their home, Uppercross Cottage, seven miles away.

'I am more than a little unwell!' Mary claimed, 'And it would make me so happy if Anne was to come and stay here for as long as she wants to, before going to Bath. I simply cannot do without Anne!'

And Elizabeth's reply was, 'Then I'm sure Anne had better stay, for nobody will want her in Bath.'

Anne was happy and relieved to accept Mary's invitation, and delay her journey to Bath. So it was arranged that she would stay with her sister until Lady Russell returned from her visit to Scotland. Anne would then be Lady Russell's guest for a few weeks until after Christmas, and then they would travel together to Bath.

Kellynch Hall
Uppercross Cottage
Kellynch Lodge
BATH

Everything seemed to be working out perfectly until Anne and Lady Russell discovered that Elizabeth had invited her friend Mrs Clay to go to Bath with herself and Sir Walter.

'Mrs Clay will be a great help to us,' Elizabeth said impatiently when Lady Russell dared to question her. Lady Russell said no more, but she was very annoyed that Penelope Clay was invited as a special guest, while Elizabeth cared nothing for Anne, her own sister.

Anne was also anxious about Penelope Clay and Sir Walter. It would be a huge scandal if her father decided to marry Mrs Clay, who, as the daughter of a man who worked for him, was of a much lower social status. Anne decided she must speak to Elizabeth on the subject. She had to gather all her courage to do so, but only seemed to offend.

'I can assure you that Mrs Clay is to be trusted completely,' Elizabeth snapped, her face red with anger. 'She understands better than anyone else that a gentleman should only marry someone from his own class. And besides, have you not heard our father talk about Mrs Clay's teeth and her freckles and how clumsy she is? There is no danger there, I'm sure.'

Anne said no more, glad the conversation was over. But she hoped that from now on, Elizabeth might be a little more watchful whenever Mrs Clay and Sir Walter were together.

CHAPTER FOUR

A week later, Anne and Lady Russell travelled to Uppercross Cottage in Lady Russell's carriage. Anne was to be left with Mary and her family, and then Lady Russell would continue directly on her journey to Scotland.

Neither Anne nor Lady Russell was in good spirits. Sir Walter, Elizabeth and Mrs Clay had already left for Bath, and *they* had been in excellent spirits, laughing and talking and looking forward to the journey. Lady Russell was very distressed by the break-up of the family and found it painful to see the empty house and gardens of Kellynch Hall, as did Anne. They were both glad to be leaving the village of Kellynch a few weeks before the Crofts moved in.

When they reached Uppercross, Anne said a fond goodbye to Lady Russell and stepped down from the carriage. Uppercross Cottage was very pretty, with French windows opening out on to a veranda, and roses and apple trees in the garden. A little way off, Anne could see the Great House with its high walls, gates and tall chimneys. Charles's parents, Mr and Mrs Musgrove, and his brothers and sisters lived there.

Anne had stayed with Mary and Charles many times before, and she knew the ways of both houses. The two families were always meeting, running in and out of each other's homes at all hours. So Anne was quite surprised to find her sister Mary all alone.

'So, here you are at last!' Mary remarked bitterly as Anne was shown into the drawing room. She was lying on the sofa, resting her head on a cushion.

'I began to think I should never see you. I am so ill, I can hardly speak! I have been on my own all morning.'

'I'm sorry you are unwell, Mary,' Anne replied gently.

'I don't believe I was ever so ill in my life!'

Mary moaned, a hand pressed to her head. 'Charles has gone out. I have not seen him since seven o'clock. He would go, even though I told him how ill I was, and now it is almost one. I have not seen a single soul all morning!'

'Not even your boys?'

'Oh, I had little Charles and Walter with me for as long as I could stand their noise,' Mary replied weakly. 'Then I asked their nanny to take them away.'

'Well, you know you always feel better when I visit,' Anne said with a comforting smile. 'And have you seen no one from the Great House this morning?'

'No one!' Mary exclaimed dramatically. 'Well, only Mr Musgrove. He was on his horse and he just stopped and spoke to me through the window. He didn't even get *off* his horse. Oh, Anne, I have been so very unwell!'

As usual, Anne set herself the task of raising

Mary's spirits. Mary soon looked more cheerful, and she sat up on the sofa. Then she began busying herself around the room, arranging the flowers. When she and Anne had lunch, she ate with a good appetite.

'Shall we go for a little walk?' Mary suggested after the meal. 'We could go to the Great House, unless you wish to wait for them to call on you here first?'

'I should be very happy to see the Musgroves,' Anne replied. 'I know them all so well.'

The two of them walked over to the Great House, where they received a warm welcome. Anne was very fond of Mary's in-laws, Mr and Mrs Musgrove, and their numerous children. Only three of the children were grown up – Mary's husband, Charles, and his two sisters Henrietta and Louisa. The girls were pretty and lively, aged nineteen and twenty, and Anne envied the easy-going, friendly relationship they had with each other. It was so different to what she had known with both of her own sisters.

Anne knew she would be questioned about what had been happening at Kellynch Hall. Sure enough, as soon as she sat down, Mrs Musgrove said, 'So, Miss Anne, your father and sister have gone to Bath?' She was a large, jolly lady whose main interest was her children, but she was also very fond of Anne. 'And what part of Bath do you think they will live in?'

'Mama, shall we go to Bath this winter?' cried Henrietta, not giving Anne a chance to reply.

'If we do, we must rent a good house, Papa,' Louisa added.

'To be sure, my dear, we will,' Mr Musgrove replied, bouncing one of his younger children on his knee.

'Upon my word, I shall be left alone when you are all gone away to be happy in Bath!' Mary remarked sulkily.

Anne smiled a little to herself. Although Mary was sometimes annoying, she was much easier to get along with than Elizabeth, and Anne was very much looking forward to being part of the noisy, lively Musgrove family during her visit. Mary's husband, Charles, was a good-humoured gentleman, Anne loved her two little nephews, and she knew that she'd enjoy spending time with the rest of the Musgroves at the Great House.

However, after a few days, Anne once again began to see the downside of visiting the two families. It happened whenever she came to stay at Uppercross – everyone tried to involve her in their arguments!

'I wish you could persuade Mary not to be always thinking herself ill,' Charles would remark to Anne, while Mary would say, 'Anne, can you not tell Charles that I am really sick, much more ill than I ever confess?'

Meanwhile, Mrs Musgrove complained to Anne about how naughty Mary's two little boys were. Then Mary would complain that Mrs Musgrove gave them too many sweets and made them ill. And when Mary was being a little annoying, Louisa and Henrietta would ask Anne to point this out to her sister. Anne could do nothing but listen patiently, and try to help as best she could.

The first three weeks of Anne's visit passed quickly. Then came the day when the Crofts were to move into Kellynch Hall. Anne could not think of much else all day, and Mary did not help by

exclaiming, 'Is this not the day that the Crofts come to Kellynch? How low that makes me!'

But Mary's curiosity was more overwhelming than her distress, and she would not rest until she had talked Charles into driving her over to visit the Crofts.

Anne, however, was glad to stay at Uppercross, since she would have found it difficult to see another family living in her beloved home. But she, too, was curious to know what the Crofts were like. Her wish was granted when they returned Mary and Charles's visit just a few days later.

While Admiral Croft played with Mary's little boys, Anne sat beside Mrs Croft. She studied Captain Wentworth's sister keenly, looking for a likeness in her face or voice. Mrs Croft was a bright-eyed, agreeable woman with a pleasant manner, and Anne liked her very much. She had been certain that Mrs Croft knew nothing of her brother's and Anne's short engagement. So it was rather a shock when Mrs Croft said, 'I believe you knew my brothers slightly when they were in Monkford?'

Anne could not reply. She could only blush and nod.

'Perhaps you have not heard – one of my brothers is recently married,' Mrs Croft added.

Anne hoped against hope that Mrs Croft wasn't speaking of her Frederick. She longed to know, but dared not ask.

Then, as the Crofts were preparing to leave, Anne saw the Admiral turn to Mary.

'We are expecting Mrs Croft's brother to visit us at Kellynch soon,' he began. But the conversation was cut short before Anne could find out any more.

A shaken and anxious Anne was left with the same question running around inside her head. Had the Admiral been speaking of her former husband-to-be, or the other Wentworth brother?

CHAPTER FIVE

Anne was soon to find out. Mr and Mrs Musgrove, Henrietta and Louisa were coming to dinner that evening at Uppercross Cottage. Louisa arrived ahead of the others on foot.

'The others are coming in the carriage,' she told Anne, Charles and Mary breathlessly. 'I wanted to warn you that Mama is not herself today. When the Crofts called on us this morning, they said that Mrs Croft's brother, Captain Frederick Wentworth, is coming to stay with them.'

Anne's heart missed a beat. She was glad the room was dark, lit only by the soft glow of the candles.

'Mama then remembered that poor Richard's captain was called Captain Wentworth,' Louisa continued. She turned to Anne. 'Richard was my brother,' Louisa explained. 'He was a sailor, and died at sea quite a while ago. Mama thinks this Wentworth may have been his captain, and so her head has been full of poor Richard all day.'

'Then we must cheer her up,' Charles replied. 'I wonder if it *is* the same Captain Wentworth?'

'It would be curious, indeed,' Louisa replied. 'You know him, Anne, do you not?'

'Yes, a little,' Anne replied, glad that no one suspected the truth.

When the other Musgroves arrived, most of the evening was spent discussing Richard and Captain Wentworth. Anne had to steel herself not to blush every time Frederick's name was mentioned. Then a few days later, they received word that Captain Wentworth had arrived at Kellynch Hall, and Mr Musgrove rode there to call on him. He invited

Captain Wentworth to dinner, and Anne had to face the fact that she and Frederick would probably be meeting each other again very soon. The thought both excited and upset her. What would he look like after eight years? Would he have changed? How would he behave towards her? And how should she behave towards *him?*

Upstairs in her room at Uppercross Cottage, Anne could think of little else. She and Mary were going over to the Great House very soon to take afternoon tea with Mrs Musgrove, Henrietta and Louisa, but Anne secretly wished she could stay at home. Her mind was full of Captain Frederick Wentworth.

Suddenly a loud thud was heard downstairs, followed by a hysterical scream from Mary. Wondering what was wrong, Anne gathered up her long skirt and ran from the room.

To her horror, Anne found little Charles lying on the floor at the bottom of the staircase, sobbing with pain. Mary and the nanny were bending over him with white, shocked faces.

'Little Charles fell down the stairs!' Mary cried, grabbing at her sister's arm. 'He was trying to slide down the banister, and he fell off and tumbled all the way to the bottom! Oh, Anne, is he going to die?'

Anne knelt down beside her nephew. 'You poor little darling, Charles!' she said kindly. 'You will be fine, I am sure. But you must lie still until the doctor gets here.' She spoke in a low voice to the nanny. 'Quickly, send one of the maids to fetch the doctor. And another must go to find Mr Charles. Keep Walter upstairs in the nursery out of the way, Jemima. Oh, and a message must be sent to the Great House. We shall not be going to tea today.'

Anne took charge of everything, but had a struggle to calm Mary down. A short while later, Charles rushed home, very worried about his son, and the doctor arrived soon afterwards. After checking little Charles carefully, he told them that the boy had dislocated his collarbone. He would recover quickly, but would need rest and peace and quiet.

Everyone was full of relief, including little Charles' grandparents, Mr and Mrs Musgrove, and his aunts, Henrietta and Louisa. They all arrived at the cottage to visit him.

'Poor little Charles!' Henrietta remarked tenderly. 'I am so glad he will soon recover! But what a pity you and Anne did not come to the Great House for tea this afternoon, Mary. If you had, you would have met Captain Wentworth, Mrs Croft's brother.'

Anne almost gasped with surprise, but managed to bite her lip to hold it back.

'Yes, he came to return Papa's visit,' Louisa added, her eyes shining. 'And he's agreed to dine with us tomorrow.'

'He is so very handsome,' Henrietta sighed.

'Yes, our heads were quite turned by him!' Louisa giggled as they followed their parents into the drawing room.

'You will probably not wish to join us for dinner tomorrow night after little Charles's accident?' Mr Musgrove said to his son, and Charles shook his head.

'Certainly not, Father. We must stay here.'

'We could not *think* of leaving our little boy while he is so ill!' Mary cried, dabbing at her eyes with a lace handkerchief.

'No, indeed,' Anne could not help adding. She was relieved that not only had she missed seeing Frederick Wentworth that very afternoon, but also that she would not have to sit down to dinner with him tomorrow evening. She wasn't sure how in command of herself she would be at seeing him again. And yet, she had to admit that she was very curious to see if he had changed at all . . .

By the following day, however, things had changed. Little Charles was recovering well. The boy was so much better that his father decided he *would* go to dinner at the Great House and meet Captain Wentworth, after all. But when he told his wife, Mary was not at all pleased.

'So!' she said grumpily to Anne. 'You and I are to be left here with poor little Charles while everyone else is enjoying themselves. This is just my luck.'

'Why don't you go to the Great House with your husband, then?' Anne urged her. 'I can stay here and look after my nephew.'

Mary cheered up instantly. 'That is an excellent idea, Anne! I shall go and change my clothes directly.'

Left alone with little Charles, Anne wondered what Captain Wentworth was thinking and feeling. He had long ago stopped loving her, of that she was sure. If he still cared for her, he could have come back after he'd made his fortune and asked her once more to marry him. Sir Walter and Lady Russell could not have objected then.

When Mary and Charles returned from dinner, they were as delighted with Captain Wentworth as the rest of the family had been. Anne hung on every word they said about him, even though she knew there was no point. Frederick Wentworth was lost to her for ever.

Next morning Anne and Mary were finishing breakfast when Charles popped his head around the door. 'Captain Wentworth rode over from Kellynch early this morning,' he announced. 'And he and my sisters are coming to say good morning on their way to the village.'

A rush of different emotions – fear, joy, excitement, panic – almost overwhelmed Anne. She rose to her feet as Louisa and Henrietta entered

the breakfast room, chattering and laughing together as usual. And behind the two Miss Musgroves was a tall, dark, handsome man who met Anne's gaze with his own. It was Captain Frederick Wentworth, looking almost exactly the same as the last time Anne had seen him eight years ago.

Anne could hardly catch her breath and had to fight to appear calm. Captain Wentworth bowed coolly to her, and she nodded her head in return, but said nothing. She could not have spoken at that moment, anyway. She was too choked with emotion.

The dining room was full of people and laughter and voices, but Anne only had eyes for Frederick Wentworth. He greeted her sister Mary and then asked how little Charles was. Just a few moments' more conversation, and then everyone was gone. Charles had decided to walk down to the village with his sisters and Captain Wentworth, and so Mary and Anne were alone again.

'It is over!' Anne repeated to herself again and again. 'The worst is over!' But her head and her heart were both turned upside down, and she could not calm herself, could not listen to Mary talking, could not finish her breakfast. How silly she was, Anne scolded herself. After eight years, she should be more in control of her feelings.

But as Anne very quickly realised, eight years meant nothing at all if one was still in love . . .

Later that morning, Henrietta and Louisa called in at the cottage again, having left Captain Wentworth and their brother looking at horses at the village stables. Anne was busy with little Charles upstairs and did not see them, but after they'd left, Mary came looking for her.

'Anne, you will never believe what Captain Wentworth said about you!' Mary announced. 'Henrietta asked him what he thought of you, and he replied that you were so much changed, he would never have known you. Well! Was that not rather unkind of him?'

Anne couldn't help feeling upset. Nevertheless, it was the simple truth. She knew she was no longer the young girl Frederick Wentworth had fallen in love with. *He* was the same – the same handsome, clever, energetic and lively man she remembered so well. But it was clear his heart no longer belonged to her.

CHAPTER SIX

From this time on, Anne and Frederick were in each other's company almost every day. Little Charles was recovering fast, so Anne had no excuse to remain at the cottage with him instead of visiting the Great House, and Captain Wentworth was often there. He began riding over from Kellynch to see the Musgroves whenever he could. The reason he gave was that he was a little bored staying at Kellynch Hall with his sister and Admiral Croft. They were so busy getting to know their new home and driving around their estate that Captain Wentworth hardly saw them. So it was Uppercross for him almost every day.

But although Anne and Frederick were together regularly, they never spoke to each other. Once they'd been so much to each other, Anne thought sadly, and now they were nothing. They were like strangers.

Anne could see that Henrietta and Louisa were charmed by him. They hardly had eyes for anyone else, and they hung on Captain Wentworth's every word when he spoke of his life in the navy on board one of his ships, HMS *Laconia*. He had been invited to dinner again, along with the Crofts and some relations of the Musgroves, the Hayters, who lived nearby.

'It was a lucky day for us, sir, when you were put in charge of the *Laconia*,' Mrs Musgrove murmured sadly.

'Mama is thinking of our poor brother Richard,' Henrietta whispered to Captain Wentworth. He understood immediately and went to sit beside Mrs Musgrove on the sofa. Anne, who was sitting on the other side of Mrs Musgrove, felt herself trembling. It was ridiculous to shake like a leaf just because he and she were sitting on the same sofa. She tried to calm herself as she listened to Frederick's familiar voice very close to her as he talked with Mrs Musgrove about her memories of her dead son.

He was still the same kindly, generous man that

Anne remembered so well. This thought gave her both pleasure and pain.

That particular evening ended with a dance. The drawing-room carpets were rolled back and the piano was opened. Anne offered to play so the others could dance, and her kindness was gratefully accepted. She seated herself at the piano and struck up a lively tune while the others took their partners.

And if her eyes sometimes filled with tears as she played, she made sure no one could see.

It was a noisy, joyful party and Captain Wentworth was in high spirits. Anne could see that, even after such a short time, he was already a great favourite with the Musgroves. The attention of all the young women – Henrietta, Louisa and their female relatives, the Hayters – was fixed on him. He was an object of huge admiration. Frederick seemed to be enjoying the attention, and who could blame him?

These were some of Anne's thoughts as her fingers flew over the piano keyboard. Once, she felt sure that Frederick was looking at her. He was staring intently in her direction as he danced with Louisa. And once, she knew that he must have spoken of her. Anne did not hear what he said, but she caught Louisa's reply.

'Oh no, Anne never dances now. She has quite given up dancing. She would rather play for us.

She never gets tired of *that*.'

Then, at last, Frederick spoke to Anne directly for the first time. The dancing was over, and she had left her seat at the piano. When she returned a little while later to collect her music sheets, Frederick was sitting on the piano stool, picking out a few notes.

'This is the song I was thinking of,' he told Henrietta and Louisa and some of the other ladies who were gathered around him. He played a few more notes, then noticed Anne standing close by. Swiftly he stood up.

'I beg your pardon, madam,' he said politely. 'This is your seat.'

'Not at all,' Anne replied. She controlled herself so well that her voice hardly shook at all. 'I have just come to collect my music. Please do not move on my account.'

But Frederick walked away from the piano immediately without another word. The ladies followed him, leaving Anne alone in the corner. So they had finally spoken. But Anne had no wish for more such conversation. Frederick's cold, polite tone and indifferent look was more than she could bear. *It would be better to stay out of his way and not speak at all*, she thought miserably.

'I *had* intended to leave Kellynch after a visit of a few days,' Captain Wentworth was telling Henrietta, Louisa and the other ladies when everyone had seated themselves again. 'I was planning to go to Shropshire and visit my brother Edward. He used to be vicar of Monkford near Kellynch, some eight years ago.'

Anne, her eyes on the floor, knew that Frederick must be thinking about their broken engagement all those years ago, just as she was. But she was very sure he did not feel the same pain as she did at the memory.

'However, the Admiral and my sister have pressed me to stay as long as I like,' Frederick went on. Anne saw Henrietta and Louisa exchange excited glances. 'So here I shall stay.'

Anne did not know whether to be overjoyed or distressed by this news. She had been slowly getting used to seeing Frederick so often, although it was still difficult to hide her true feelings. Perhaps, over time, the pain at observing him having fun, from across the room, would lessen?

Soon, though, Anne realised that this was only the beginning of her problems as another fact became clear: Frederick Wentworth meant to marry either Henrietta or Louisa Musgrove.

CHAPTER SEVEN

'I must say, I have never met a more pleasant man than Captain Wentworth in my life!' Charles Musgrove said to his wife Mary at breakfast the following week. 'He is a real gentleman. And from things he has said, I think he has made a great fortune.'

Anne drank her coffee in silence. She knew what was coming. Charles and Mary had talked of nothing else for the last four or five days.

'I do believe Wentworth is looking for a wife, and I think Louisa would suit him perfectly,' Charles began, as he'd already said at least twenty times. And, as she did every time, Mary interrupted him.

'Louisa!' she exclaimed scornfully. 'Not at all, my dear Charles. I have told you before – Henrietta is definitely his favourite.'

Anne did not speak. Her sister and brother-in-law had had this argument so many times already, and they would often ask her what she thought. Anne herself could not quite tell whether Frederick preferred Louisa or Henrietta best. Henrietta was the prettiest, but Louisa was more lively and playful. Anne wasn't sure which one of them Frederick might choose.

Charles was frowning at his wife. 'Come, Mary, don't be silly,' he said, taking a bite of bread and butter. 'You know very well that Henrietta is to marry Charles Hayter.'

'There has been no official engagement yet!' Mary cried. 'And I very much hope there never will be. Charles Hayter is only a farmer! It would be a very bad match for Henrietta.'

Anne knew that Charles Hayter, a distant relative of the Musgroves, hoped to make Henrietta

his wife. She had seen them together when she'd visited Uppercross previously, and it had seemed to Anne that Henrietta had felt the same way. But Charles Hayter had been away on business since Frederick Wentworth had arrived, and Henrietta's feelings seemed to have changed.

'You are talking nonsense, Mary,' Charles

Musgrove retorted, looking quite annoyed. 'Charles Hayter is a perfectly respectable gentleman farmer. No, if Henrietta marries Hayter and Louisa can get Captain Wentworth, I shall be very well satisfied.'

He left the breakfast room, and Mary rolled her eyes at Anne. 'Well, Charles can say what he pleases,' she muttered. 'But why should I, the daughter of Sir Walter Elliot, be expected to meet with a *farmer*? Henrietta can do much better for herself, and Captain Wentworth is the man for her, believe me.'

'Do you think so, Mary?' Anne asked softly. She had already realised that the announcement of Frederick's wedding to either Henrietta or Louisa would be the unhappiest day of her life.

Mary nodded. 'I do. Charles Hayter was at dinner with us at the Great House yesterday, and Henrietta hardly took any notice of him. She only spoke to Captain Wentworth.' As usual,

Anne had been invited to the dinner too, but she'd had a headache and stayed at home, partly to avoid Frederick. Now she was glad that she had. She did feel sorry for Charles Hayter, though. He and Henrietta had seemed so perfectly suited.

I hope Frederick makes up his mind quickly between the two sisters, Anne thought, rising from her seat as the maid came to clear the breakfast dishes. *Either of them will make him a good wife, I suppose.* But she hoped that no announcement would be made until she had left for Bath. Then, at a distance, she might be able to bear it.

Later that morning, Anne was in the drawing room with little Charles. The boy was still recovering from his accident, but he was now allowed downstairs and Anne was making him comfortable on the sofa. Suddenly one of the maids opened the door, and Frederick Wentworth unexpectedly walked in.

Both he and Anne were taken completely by surprise. They were alone in the room except for little Charles, who was almost asleep, and at first, neither of them could speak. Anne blushed with embarrassment and Frederick seemed lost for words.

'I am sorry,' he said awkwardly at last. 'I thought the Musgrove sisters were here. Mrs Musgrove told me I should find them here.' And he walked over to the window and stood there, as if trying to calm himself.

'They *are* here,' Anne replied. 'They are upstairs with my sister. They will all be down in a moment.' She would have quickly left the room then and escaped, but the sound of their voices had woken little Charles from his doze.

'Aunt Anne, my bandage is too tight,' he said fretfully.

Anne knelt down beside the sofa and began to unwind her nephew's bandage, glad to have something to do so that she didn't have to make polite small talk with Frederick.

'I hope the little boy is better,' Captain Wentworth remarked, and after that he was silent.

A moment later, Anne heard footsteps outside in the hall and was very relieved. She thought it must be her brother-in-law, but when the maid opened the door for the second time, Anne's heart sank. To her dismay, it was Charles Hayter, and he did not look pleased to see Captain Wentworth at all. There was truth in what Mary had said at breakfast then, Anne realised. Charles Hayter was worried that Henrietta now preferred Captain Wentworth. But Anne said nothing except, 'How do you do? Will you sit down? The others will be here presently.'

Captain Wentworth turned from the window as if eager to talk to the newcomer, but Charles Hayter was having none of it. With a haughty stare, he sat down and picked up the newspaper. Anne saw that

Captain Wentworth looked a little surprised, but nothing more. He did not know, then, that Henrietta and Charles Hayter had been expected to announce their engagement, Anne thought.

The door opened again, and this time Anne's youngest nephew, Walter, toddled in. He was a sturdy, stubborn child of two years old, and he went straight to the sofa to see what was going on. Anne had no time for him as she was busy with little Charles, and Walter was annoyed. He decided it would be a good game to climb on to his favourite aunt's back and cling there like a little monkey. Anne tried to push him away, but in vain.

'Walter, you are very naughty!' she scolded, unable to do anything more as her hands were full of bandages. 'Get down this moment. I am very angry with you.'

'Walter!' Charles Hayter called, laying down his newspaper. 'Do you not hear your aunt? Leave her alone and come here.'

But Walter clung on to Anne with all his might and would not move. In fact, the attention seemed to make him more determined in his game, and he giggled loudly as tightened his arms around her.

A moment later, Anne felt someone behind her. They were removing the little boy from her back, gently unfastening his hands from around

her neck and lifting him away from her.

It was Frederick.

Anne was speechless. She could not find the words to thank Frederick for his swift action. His kindness in stepping forward to help her was so much like him. Now he was playing noisily with Walter over at the window, as if to avoid hearing Anne's thanks.

It was obvious, too, that Charles Hayter was extremely annoyed. Anne heard him say angrily, 'You should have minded me, Walter! I told you not to tease your aunt!'

Then Mary, Henrietta and Louisa came downstairs into the drawing room, all talking at once, and Anne finally had a chance to escape to her own room. She was in such a fluster, she could not have stayed. Anne was ashamed of herself, ashamed of being so overcome by such a small thing. But it was a long, long time before she managed to calm herself down.

CHAPTER EIGHT

Although Anne tried to avoid Frederick Wentworth as much as possible, she could not make excuses to escape every family party, so she had plenty of opportunities to observe Henrietta, Charles Hayter, Louisa and Frederick together at the Great House. From what Anne had seen, she did not believe that Frederick was in love with either of the sisters. Louisa was perhaps his favourite. Anne was also certain that neither Henrietta nor Louisa was in love with Frederick either. Not yet. They only liked and admired him at this moment, but it would probably end in love at some point. Charles Hayter was increasingly annoyed at being overlooked, but sometimes Henrietta seemed torn between him and Captain Wentworth. Anne only hoped the situation would sort itself out, and soon. Her nerves were in shreds.

The first move to resolve the situation was made by Charles Hayter. He simply stopped visiting the Great House and refused all invitations to dinner.

'I think Henrietta has told him she will not marry him!' Mary reported gleefully to Anne. 'You see that I was right all along! I hope it is the end of such an unsuitable relationship.'

But Anne secretly felt that Charles Hayter had made a wise move.

A few days later, on a fine November morning, Anne and Mary were sitting in the drawing room. Charles had gone out with Captain Wentworth, and the two sisters were about to spend a quiet day with their needlework. But they had only just opened their sewing boxes when Louisa and

Henrietta walked in.

'We are on our way to take a long walk and have just stopped by to say hello,' Louisa announced. 'I don't suppose you will like to come with us, Mary. We know you are not fond of a *long* walk.'

'Oh, but I love long walks!' Mary exclaimed, throwing aside her sewing. 'I will be ready directly.'

Anne noticed Henrietta and Louisa glance at each other in dismay. For some reason known only to themselves, they did not want Mary to go with them. Not for the first time, Anne was amused that the two families felt they had to share everything they were doing. Even when they didn't want the others to join them!

'Do come with us too, Anne,' Louisa urged in a much more friendly manner, and Anne agreed. She and Mary could always turn around and come back, leaving the Musgrove sisters to go on alone. Anne suspected that Henrietta and Louisa had some secret plan in mind.

Just as they were setting off, Charles and Captain Wentworth returned. They decided to join the ladies on their walk too, and so they all immediately set off across the fields. If Anne had known Frederick was to join them, then she would have refused Louisa's invitation. But it was too late to back out now, and it would look odd if she did.

Determined to enjoy the walk, Anne kept away from Frederick and stayed with Charles and Mary. She found pleasure in the clear blue skies, mellow sunshine and the gold, orange and red leaves drifting slowly down from the trees. She tried to keep her thoughts busy by remembering lines of poems she had read about the beauty of autumn days. But, whenever she was near Frederick, Henrietta and Louisa, it was impossible not to listen to what they were saying. It was nothing out of the ordinary – just lively, friendly chat. But Anne noticed that Frederick spoke more with Louisa

than with Henrietta.

'What glorious weather for the Admiral and my sister!' Frederick exclaimed, gazing up at the sky. 'They are taking a drive today around this part of the countryside, and we may come upon them while we are walking.' He smiled. 'The Admiral is a wonderful sailor, but not such a good driver. I wonder where they will overturn their carriage today? My sister makes nothing of it, though, and is willing to take her chance with him!'

'I should do just the same in her place,' Louisa said firmly. 'If I loved a man as she loves the Admiral, I would rather be overturned by him than driven safely by anybody else!'

'Would you?' Frederick cried. 'Wonderful!' And there was silence between them for a little while.

Anne heard all of this and could not easily bring her mind back to the poetry she loved. The path they were taking up the hill seemed familiar, and she asked, 'Is this not the way to the Hayters' house?'

But nobody heard, or, at least, nobody answered her.

A few moments later they reached the top of the hill, and there below them was the Hayters' farm.

'I declare, I had no idea we had come so far!' Mary said with a yawn. 'I am so very tired. We had better turn back.'

Anne could see that Henrietta was eagerly scanning the farm buildings and the fields, looking for Charles Hayter. But he was nowhere to be seen and so she turned away, ready to do as Mary wished.

'Wait, Henrietta,' Charles Musgrove told his sister firmly. 'We must go and call on our relatives now we are so near.'

'Charles is right,' Louisa said, taking her sister's arm. 'Do not turn away.' She pulled Henrietta aside, and the two of them held a whispered conversation.

'I must run down and say hello to Mr and Mrs Hayter,' Charles insisted. 'Mary, will you come too?'

'Certainly not,' Mary snapped coldly. 'I am far too tired to walk so far!' But Anne knew it was really because Mary considered the Hayters not worthy of her notice.

Charles Musgrove spoke with his two sisters, and it was decided that Charles and Henrietta would just run down to the Hayters' house for a few minutes, while the others remained behind. Henrietta was pink in the face and looked very embarrassed. Louisa walked down the hill a little way with her, talking intently all the time.

Mary was frowning sulkily. 'It is very unpleasant to have such low-born relatives,' she muttered to Captain Wentworth.

Anne saw the look of disgust on Frederick's face, but he said nothing.

Having left her brother and sister halfway down the hill, Louisa returned and they all moved to find

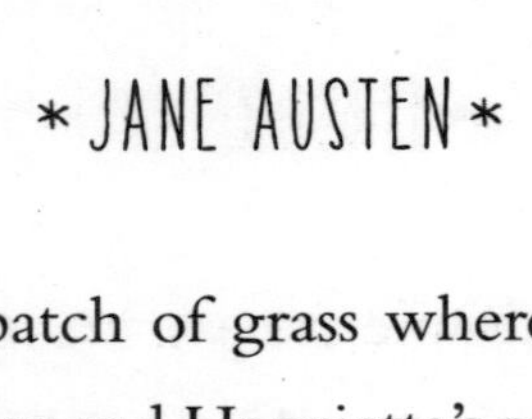

a comfortable patch of grass where they might sit and await Charles and Henrietta's return. But when Louisa drew Captain Wentworth away to search for nuts in the hedgerow, Mary was no longer happy.

'I'm sure Louisa and Captain Wentworth have found somewhere better to sit,' Mary grumbled. 'I am going to find them.' And she followed them into the field.

Alone at last, Anne felt exhausted. She was glad to stay seated in the sunshine and catch her breath. But quite soon afterwards she heard Louisa and Captain Wentworth chatting to each other as they made their way towards her on the other side of the hedgerow. They could not see Anne as she was hidden by the thick, thorny blackberry bushes between them.

'And so I made Henrietta go,' Louisa was saying. 'I could not bear her to be shamed out of visiting Charles Hayter. Would I turn away from something I was determined to do because of someone like Mary? No, *I* am not so easily persuaded!'

'So Henrietta would have turned back, but for you, then?'

'She would indeed. I am almost ashamed to say it.'

'I hope your sister and Charles Hayter work things out between them,' Anne heard Captain Wentworth remark, very sincerely. 'I had not realised they were thinking of marriage. Your sister is a gentle girl, but I see that *you* have a strength of character that she does not.' Frederick's voice became more serious as he continued, 'Let those who would be happy know their own mind and stand firm! Do not allow others to persuade you to do what you know to be the wrong course of action.'

Anne's heart swelled with pain. She knew that Frederick was thinking of how she had broken their engagement on Lady Russell's advice all those years ago. Louisa and Frederick were moving on now, and a big holly bush screened Anne from their view. But she could still hear what they were saying.

'I am fond of Mary,' Louisa remarked with a sigh, 'but sometimes she annoys me very much. She has the Elliot pride, just like her father and her sister Elizabeth. They all think they are so very important! Anne is not like that, thank goodness. We do so wish Charles had married Anne instead. I suppose you know that he wanted to marry Anne?'

There was a pause during which Anne's heart beat so loudly, she thought they must surely hear it. Then Frederick said, 'Do you mean that Anne refused your brother? When did that happen?'

'Yes, Anne said no to Charles. I do not know exactly when, because Henrietta and I were away at school. We should all have liked Anne *so* much better. Mama and Papa believe it was her great friend Lady Russell's fault. They think she persuaded Anne to refuse him.'

Their voices were growing fainter now as they walked on, and Anne heard no more. Her mind was racing here and there as different emotions overwhelmed her. She had heard nothing bad about herself, and yet she knew what Frederick Wentworth must think of her. Persuaded out of yet another marriage by Lady Russell! Anne was mortified. But what Louisa had said was not true. Lady Russell had *wanted* Anne to accept Charles Musgrove's offer of marriage. It was Anne who had refused, because there was only one man she had ever loved, and it was not Charles Musgrove.

But she was even more unsettled because of the close interest Frederick was taking in her affairs. Why was he so keen to know about her?

Mary soon appeared again, and then Louisa and

Frederick returned, with handfuls of nuts and blackberries. And finally, Charles Musgrove walked up the hill from the farmhouse, followed by Henrietta and Charles Hayter. Henrietta looked a little shy and embarrassed, but both she and Charles Hayter could not take their eyes from each other. They walked a little apart from the others, and Anne realised that they had made up and were a happy couple again.

Everything now marked Louisa out for Captain Wentworth. Nothing could be more obvious, Anne thought, trying to ignore her aching heart. Louisa and Frederick stayed together as they all walked home and did not leave each other's side. Anne walked with Charles and Mary, but Charles was annoyed with his wife for not going to visit the Hayters with him. So he and she did not talk at all. Anne stayed silent too, busy with her thoughts. She was very tired and wished she was alone at home so that she had time and space to think about everything that had happened that day.

As they crossed the lane, they heard the sound of horse's hooves. They all turned to see Admiral and Mrs Croft driving towards them in a small one-horse carriage.

'How far you have walked!' Mrs Croft observed when they had all greeted each other. 'Would any of the ladies like to ride home with us?'

'We are going past Uppercross to return to Kellynch,' the Admiral added. 'It would save one of you a walk of at least a mile. And we would be very happy to help.'

Both Louisa and Henrietta declared that they were not tired at all. Mary kept silent, probably, Anne thought, because her sister was too proud to squash herself into a small carriage that was really only meant for two people.

Then Captain Wentworth went up to his sister and murmured something to her that no one else could hear.

'Miss Anne Elliot, I am sure you are very tired!' Mrs Croft said immediately. 'Do let us have the pleasure of taking you back to Uppercross. There is room for three, I assure you. If we were all like you, I believe we might sit four! You must, indeed you must.' And she and the Admiral pressed themselves together to leave a free corner.

Anne was about to refuse politely, but Frederick took her arm without a word and helped her into the carriage. He had seen she was tired, Anne realised, and he wanted to help her. He did not care for her any longer, but he would not stand by and see her in distress. It was proof of Frederick's warm, kind heart, and brought her to the edge of tears.

'Frederick certainly means to marry one of those two girls, Sophy,' Admiral Croft remarked to his wife as they waved the others goodbye and set off in the carriage.

'A very respectable family indeed,' Mrs Croft replied calmly. 'Frederick has not said much to me about either of the girls. But he did tell me he was looking for a wife with "a strong mind and a sweetness of manner". Those were his very words.'

'Well, I wish Frederick would decide quickly,' the Admiral muttered. 'If he likes one of those girls, there's no point in waiting! I wonder what's keeping him?'

Anne said nothing, and was very glad to be put down at Uppercross Cottage a short while later. It had been a tiring day, in more ways than one, and she had a lot to think about.

CHAPTER NINE

The time was now drawing near for Lady Russell to return from Scotland and collect Anne. They were to spend a little time at Lady Russell's home in Kellynch, and then go to Bath together.

Anne realised that she would be closer to Frederick at Kellynch Hall than ever. But as he spent so much time at Uppercross with the Musgroves, Anne thought that she would probably see him less. She felt saddened to be losing him from her life once more, but knew it was for the best that she was leaving Uppercross. Anne was glad to have been useful to little Charles after his accident, but she did not wish to be with the family when Frederick announced his engagement to Louisa. That would be too much to bear.

The one thing Anne was very anxious about was the possibility of Lady Russell meeting Frederick Wentworth again, after all these years. They did not like each other, and nothing good could come of their meeting. She hoped it would not happen.

However, Anne's visit was to end in a way she could never have imagined. Frederick Wentworth was absent from Uppercross for two days, and when he returned, he explained the reason why. He had just heard that a sailor friend of his, Captain Harville, was living in Lyme, only seventeen miles from Uppercross. Captain Harville was not in good health, and Frederick was worried about him, so he had set off for Lyme immediately to visit Harville and his family.

'Lyme is such a beautiful place,' Frederick told the Musgroves, Charles, Mary and Anne at dinner when he returned. 'Not only is it on the coast, but the countryside around the town is also well worth seeing.'

'Let us all go to visit Lyme and meet Captain Wentworth's friends!' Louisa cried eagerly, dropping her knife and fork with a clatter in her excitement. 'Mary and Charles, you will come too, won't you? And Anne, of course – we must make the most of our time before you depart Uppercross!'

'But, my dear, it is November, and we must expect bad weather,' her father pointed out. 'It would not be sensible.'

'Oh, but Papa, it is so dry and bright at the moment!' Louisa exclaimed. 'It is more like August than November.'

'Could you not put off the trip until the summer?' Mrs Musgrove suggested to her daughter, but Louisa shook her head.

'No, Mama, I am determined,' she replied firmly. 'We can leave tomorrow while the weather is still fine.' And so to Lyme they were to go, Anne, Mary, Charles, Henrietta, Louisa and Captain Wentworth. They would stay the night there and not be expected back until lunchtime the following day. Anne was thrilled by this unexpected trip, and as excited to see Lyme as the others.

Next morning, they left the Great House bright and early. The ladies were travelling in the Musgroves' coach, while Charles drove Captain Wentworth in his smaller carriage. The journey was slow and they had to stop several times for the horses to eat and drink, so it was around midday when they finally reached Lyme.

Anne was struck by her first glimpse of the little town. Lyme was very pretty. It was nestled in the curve of a bay underneath cliffs that stretched along the coast. It had narrow, winding streets and a harbour called the Cobb. The Cobb had long stone walls running around it that Anne thought would make a pleasant walk with fine sea views.

She breathed in the fresh, salty air deeply, enjoying the feel of the strong breeze on her face.

The first thing to be done was to find an inn and book themselves rooms for the night. Because it was November, there were very few other visitors in Lyme, so they found somewhere to stay very easily. Having ordered dinner for that evening,

Louisa decided that they should then walk down to the sea.

'I must go and tell Harville that we are here,' Captain Wentworth said as they left the inn. 'And there is something else you should know, before you meet the Harville family.' A serious look crossed his face, and Anne wondered what he was about to say. 'They have another friend of mine, Captain James Benwick, staying with them at the moment. He has a very sad history.'

'Tell us,' Louisa said immediately.

'Benwick was to marry Harville's sister, Frances,' Frederick continued in a low voice. 'But while he was away at sea last summer, she died of pneumonia.'

'Oh, the poor man!' Henrietta exclaimed.

'James Benwick is broken up by it all.' Frederick sighed deeply. 'He has moved in with the Harvilles, but I am not sure he will ever recover from his loss. His love for Frances Harville was very strong. Now if you will excuse me, I shall go and tell Harville and

Benwick that we are here. They live near the harbour.'

'What a sad story!' Louisa said as Captain Wentworth strode off towards the Cobb.

'And what a shock it must have been for him when he returned home from sea,' Anne said softly, full of pity for the young man. The others murmured in agreement.

'Shall we walk to the harbour ourselves and wait there for Wentworth?' Charles suggested.

As they were standing on the harbour wall, enjoying the sea breeze, Anne spotted Frederick coming towards them with two men in naval uniform, and a woman. She realised quickly that the older couple must be Captain Harville and his wife, while the younger fellow was probably Captain James Benwick. His handsome face had a sad, serious expression that caught Anne's attention.

And yet perhaps Captain Benwick is no more unlucky in love than I am myself, Anne thought, observing the young man as they came closer.

The two groups met and were introduced. Anne immediately liked both of Frederick's friends. Captain Harville and Benwick were both perfect gentlemen, although Benwick was much quieter and did not seem to want to talk much to anyone. Mrs Harville was as pleasant and welcoming as her husband, and all three of them seemed to think a great deal of Frederick Wentworth.

If Frederick and I had married, these people would all have been my *friends too*, Anne thought sadly, and she had to struggle against feeling very low.

They all decided to stroll along the harbour wall together, and as they walked, Anne found herself next to Captain Benwick.

'Tell me, how do you like Lyme?' she asked him gently.

'Very much, thank you.' Captain Benwick was rather shy and did not say any more, but Anne did not give up. With a few well-chosen questions, she discovered that James Benwick was a great reader.

He very much enjoyed reading poetry, as did Anne, and soon they were talking together like old friends. They discussed their favourite poems, as well as the novels they liked best, and Anne decided that Captain Benwick was a very pleasant young man. She was sure that one day he would find someone to replace his lost love.

After a good dinner, Anne and the others spent a comfortable night at the inn. Anne rose early, as she usually did, and she and Henrietta decided to take a stroll on the beach until the others woke up. As they enjoyed the crisp salty air, they met Captain Wentworth and Louisa, who had come to look for them, and they all set off back to the inn.

'The Harvilles and Benwick will come to meet us after breakfast,' Frederick told them. 'We can take our last walk around Lyme with them before we leave for Uppercross.'

When they reached the steps leading up from the beach, a gentleman at the top stopped there to allow them to climb up first. As Anne passed him with a murmured 'thank you', the man stared admiringly at her. Anne was pink-cheeked and bright-eyed from the sea breezes, and was looking her best. She couldn't help noticing that the gentleman was staring at her, but she blushed a little when she realised that Frederick had noticed this too.

Back at the inn, Anne went up to her room to take off her hat and coat before breakfast. As she hurried out again, she almost bumped into someone outside her door. As she apologised, she was extremely surprised to see the very same gentleman from the beach.

'No, please allow me to apologise to *you*, madam,' the man said with a smile. 'I am to blame, I assure you.'

What a very well-mannered man! Anne thought as she continued her way downstairs. *He is both attractive and agreeable. I wonder who he is?*

Anne joined the others in the dining room.

They had almost finished breakfast when the clatter of a carriage on the cobbles in the yard drew their attention.

'Is a new guest arriving?' Charles Musgrove asked the waiter.

'No, sir, a gentleman is leaving today,' he replied.

Curious, Anne, Charles and the others moved to the window. There they watched as the same

man Anne had just bumped into came outside and climbed into his smart carriage.

'It is the man we saw at the beach,' Frederick remarked, with a glance at Anne. He turned to the waiter. 'Can you tell us the name of that gentleman who has just left?'

'Yes, sir, his name is Mr William Elliot,' the waiter replied. 'His coachman told me that Mr Elliot is a very rich man, and that he will inherit a title and lots of land one day.'

'Elliot!' everyone gasped, even before the waiter had finished speaking.

'Anne, that is our relative, Mr William Elliot!' Mary cried, her eyes sparkling with excitement. 'Oh, what a shame we did not know. We could have spoken to him before we left.'

Anne kept quiet about having bumped into Mr Elliot just before breakfast. She would never hear the end of it from Mary if she told her.

'Anne, you must write to Bath and tell Papa

and Elizabeth that we have seen Mr Elliot,' Mary told her sister as they left the dining room together after breakfast. 'Papa will be interested, I'm sure.'

'Mary, you know that Papa and Mr Elliot are no longer on speaking terms,' Anne reminded her patiently. She was secretly pleased that her father's heir appeared to be a perfect gentleman with an air of good sense about him, but she did not intend to mention Mr William Elliot to either Sir Walter or Elizabeth. Her father and sister were annoyed at even the very thought of Mr Elliot after his rude behaviour to them years earlier.

When the Harvilles and Captain Benwick arrived, they all set out for a long walk. Captain Benwick quickly found his way to Anne's side again, and they began to talk of books once more. But when they changed direction, the group shifted places, and Anne ended up walking next to Captain Harville.

'My dear Miss Elliot,' Captain Harville said,

speaking rather low, 'you have done a kind thing, talking with Captain Benwick so much. You have been great company for him.'

'He is an excellent young man,' Anne observed gently. 'He will need time to recover from his loss. I believe it only happened last summer?'

Captain Harville sighed and nodded. 'Benwick was away at sea when my poor sister breathed her last, but when I got news that he was returning home, I could not tell him! I simply could not do it.' He glanced at Captain Wentworth and lowered his voice even more. 'So that dear fellow Frederick decided to row out to meet Benwick's ship as it sailed into the harbour. He broke the bad news to James, and then he stayed with him for a week, never leaving him day or night! You can guess how much Frederick means to us all, Miss Anne.'

Anne could indeed guess, and her own heart was so full of love and pride she could hardly speak. They'd now reached the Harvilles' house, and they all said their final goodbyes.

'It is time we returned to the inn,' Charles said, taking out his pocket watch. 'We must start our journey home. My parents will be expecting us.'

'Oh, surely not so soon, dearest Charles!' Louisa smiled at her brother. 'We must have one last walk around the Cobb. I insist!'

'Musgrove is right,' Captain Wentworth said. 'We really should go.' But Louisa was so determined that at last the two men agreed.

'In that case, I will go with you,' Captain Benwick said, moving to Anne's side once more. The Harvilles went into their house, and the others set off around the harbour walls again.

The wind was much stronger than the day before. The gentlemen had to hold on to their hats, and the ladies to their skirts. Eventually, they all agreed to move from the higher wall down to the lower, where it would be more sheltered. One by one, they carefully climbed down the steep flight of steps, Anne holding on to Captain Benwick's arm. But Louisa paused halfway up the steps.

'Captain Wentworth must jump me down them!' she insisted, laughing merrily. 'Just as he does when I jump down from stiles on our country walks!'

'My dear Louisa, it is too dangerous,' Frederick protested. 'The stone is very hard for your feet.'

But Louisa was having none of it. She held out her hands and jumped down the steps with Frederick's help. Then, to show how much she'd enjoyed it, she instantly ran up the steps to do it again.

'No, Louisa!' Frederick exclaimed. 'Once is quite enough.'

Louisa smiled. 'I am determined I will!' she cried.

Frederick held out his hands, but he was too late – Louisa had already jumped, and without his support, she tumbled down the steps on to the stone pavement and lay there without moving.

CHAPTER TEN

The horror of that moment could not be described. At first, no one could move or speak as they stared at Louisa in shock. There was no wound, no blood, no bruises, but Louisa was hardly breathing and her face was white as chalk. And still she did not open her eyes, even when Frederick, his face as pale as hers, knelt down beside her.

'She is dead!' Mary screamed, clinging on to her husband's arm. 'Louisa is dead!'

Henrietta was so upset by Mary's words, she almost fainted. Anne and Captain Benwick caught her arms as she collapsed and held her up between them.

'Can no one help me?' Frederick burst out despairingly as he wrapped Louisa in his arms.

'Go to him,' Anne told Captain Benwick. 'I can support Henrietta myself. Rub Louisa's hands, keep her warm with your jacket, do not allow her to get cold. Here are my smelling salts. Take them, take them.'

Captain Benwick immediately did as Anne said. Charles sat a sobbing Mary down on the wall and rushed over to join them. Captain Benwick waved the bottle of smelling salts gently under Louisa's nose, but she remained unconscious.

'Oh, God!' Frederick exclaimed painfully. 'Her mother and father!'

'A doctor!' cried Anne.

Frederick caught her words. 'Yes, a doctor! We need a doctor immediately.' He gave Louisa into her brother's care and jumped to his feet, but Anne said quickly, 'Would it not be better for Captain Benwick to go? He knows where a doctor can be found.'

Captain Benwick did not argue. He was gone in an instant, leaving Louisa with Charles and Captain Wentworth. Charles, who loved his sisters dearly, watched anxiously over Louisa with tears rolling down his cheeks. Meanwhile Anne did her best to calm Mary down and to support Henrietta, who was still clinging to her.

'Anne, what is to be done?' Charles groaned

helplessly. 'What in heaven's name is to be done next?' Frederick, too, was staring at Anne in a panic.

'Shall we carry her carefully to the inn?' Anne suggested. 'Yes, I am sure that would be best.'

'Yes, yes, to the inn,' Frederick repeated. 'I will carry her there myself. Musgrove, take care of the others.'

A crowd had gathered on the wall by this time, and some of these people stepped forward to help Anne support Henrietta, who was still reeling with shock and fear. Charles took charge of Mary and, with Captain Wentworth carrying Louisa, they set off to return to the inn with heavy hearts.

They had not gone far when they saw the Harvilles running to meet them. From their window they had seen Captain Benwick rushing past and had realised that something was wrong.

'The poor girl!' Captain Harville murmured sympathetically. 'Bring her into our house immediately, Frederick.'

'But—' Frederick began.

'Yes, indeed,' Mrs Harville insisted. 'She must be put straight to bed before the doctor arrives.'

While she was being carried upstairs in the Harvilles' house, Louisa opened her eyes once. She closed them again without saying anything, but this was enough for Henrietta.

'She is alive!' Henrietta gasped, bursting into tears of joy as she clung to Anne's arm.

The doctor was soon with them. Everyone, including Anne, was sick with worry as he examined Louisa, but at last he came downstairs to speak to them.

'It is a bad head wound,' the doctor told them gravely, 'but it is not the worst I have ever seen. I have high hopes of a full recovery.'

Anne would never forget the expression on Frederick's face when he heard this. 'Thank God!' he muttered, hiding his face in his hands.

They now had to decide what to do for the best. It was clear that Louisa would have to remain where she was, even though the Harvilles' home was only small. They had four children of their own, and also Captain Benwick was staying with them, so it would be a tight squeeze. Captain Benwick immediately offered to find himself a room elsewhere, but the house would still be very crowded if anyone else wanted to stay there with Louisa.

In the Harvilles' drawing room, Frederick, Charles and Henrietta put their heads together and tried to agree what they should do. Anne was upstairs helping Mrs Harville with Louisa, and Mary, complaining of a headache, was lying down quietly in one of the other bedrooms. But when Anne came downstairs, she caught part of the conversation in the drawing room.

'We are agreed, then, that someone must return to Uppercross to break the bad news to your parents,' Frederick was saying urgently. 'We should have left here an hour ago, and there is not a moment to waste. Musgrove, either you or I must go.'

'I agree,' Charles replied, 'But I cannot leave my sister.'

'And I must stay, too,' Henrietta said weakly. 'I will help Mrs Harville look after Louisa.'

'My dear Henrietta, you cannot be in the same room as Louisa without bursting into tears,' Charles pointed out gently. 'And someone will need to be at home to comfort our mother and father when they hear this upsetting news.'

'Very well,' Henrietta agreed at last. 'I will go.'

'Then it is settled, Musgrove,' Frederick said to Charles. 'We will leave at once. Only one person needs to stay to help Mrs Harville with Louisa. I am sure your wife will want to get home to her children, so she can return with us. But if Anne will stay – no one better or more suitable than Anne!'

Anne was standing in the doorway as Frederick spoke, and he stared eagerly at her. She blushed deeply at the look in his eyes.

'I am very happy to stay,' she murmured. 'All I need is a bed on the floor of Louisa's room. That is enough.'

'Then it is agreed. I will hire a faster carriage at the inn, and return as soon as I can.' Frederick grabbed his hat and strode over to the door. 'Make sure Henrietta and your wife are ready to leave the instant I return.' He closed the front door behind him.

'Where is Captain Wentworth going?' asked Mary, yawning as she came down the stairs.

'To the inn to hire a faster carriage, my dear,' Charles replied. 'You and Henrietta are to return with him to Uppercross as soon as possible.'

'What!' Mary cried, much to Anne's dismay. 'I do not believe my ears! Why am I to be sent away instead of Anne? I am Louisa's sister-in-law, and I should stay here to look after her. Anne is nothing to Louisa. And to go home without my husband, too? Charles, you cannot be so unkind!'

Anne could not say a word as Mary kept on complaining loudly, and even managed a few tears. In the end, Charles gave in. Mary would stay, and Anne would leave with Frederick and Henrietta.

Anne was extremely concerned about the arrangement but could do nothing about it. While they waited for Frederick to return with the carriage, she said her goodbyes to the Harvilles and to Captain Benwick.

'I am sorry our short friendship has ended in this manner,' Captain Benwick said, bowing over her hand. 'But I hope we meet again.'

'And so do I,' Anne replied with a smile.

When Captain Wentworth arrived with the carriage, he was surprised and very annoyed when Charles told him that Mary was staying in place of Anne. But like Anne, he could say nothing.

Instead he handed Henrietta and Anne into the carriage, and they set off for Uppercross without delay. Anne was a little anxious about the long journey in Frederick's company, but he devoted himself very kindly to Henrietta. He tried to keep her spirits up, even though it was a difficult task.

'Poor Louisa,' Henrietta said softly, tears beginning to fall again. 'How I wish we had never taken that last walk!'

'Oh, don't talk of it!' Frederick cried. 'If only I had not given way to her! But she was so determined. Her mind was quite made up. Dear, sweet Louisa!'

Sitting silently in a corner of the carriage, Anne couldn't help but wonder if Frederick might change his views slightly now. Perhaps firmness of character and never changing one's mind was not *always* the best way?

The journey passed very quickly. Before long, Anne was able to recognise the countryside around them, and she knew they were not far from Uppercross. Henrietta had cried herself to sleep, and Anne and Frederick sat in silence as they drew near to the Great House. Finally, Frederick spoke to Anne in a low voice.

'I have been thinking what we should do,' he said. 'I don't think Henrietta should come in, at first. Will you wait in the carriage with her while I go inside and break the news to the Musgroves? Do you think this is a good plan?'

'A very good plan,' Anne whispered. Frederick looked satisfied, and she was pleased. It was a proof of their new friendship that he valued her opinion, even though he was no longer in love with her.

CHAPTER ELEVEN

Anne remained at Uppercross for only two more days. She spent all her time at the Great House, keeping Mr and Mrs Musgrove and Henrietta company. They were all desperately worried about Louisa and waited anxiously for news about how she was. But she appeared to be much the same, and was still unconscious.

'The doctor does not think Louisa will recover quickly,' Charles told them the next day. He had driven over from Lyme very early that morning to give them the latest report. 'But it is almost certain that she *will* get better. Mrs Harville is an excellent nurse. And really, she does not need Mary's or anyone's help.'

Charles returned to Lyme that very same afternoon. The following day, Charles Hayter rode his horse from Uppercross to Lyme to find out if there was any change. He brought better news back with him.

'Louisa is slowly becoming stronger,' he informed them. 'She is awake now, and seems to understand what is going on.'

'Thank heavens!' Mrs Musgrove exclaimed, wiping tears from her eyes. 'You have saved her life, Anne. We heard how you helped her after she fell.'

But the family could not bear being away from Louisa, not knowing how she was doing every hour, so it was decided they would all travel to Lyme and find lodgings there. That way they could help Mrs Harville by looking after her children while she cared for Louisa.

Anne helped them with their packing, then saw them off in the carriage the following morning.

The Great House was now empty, with the Musgroves in Lyme and their younger children away at boarding school. Anne was alone at the cottage, except for her two little nephews and their nanny. Lady Russell was due to collect her that day, and Anne stood at the window, waiting for her. Watching the raindrops beat against the glass, she was now certain that, when Louisa recovered, she and Frederick Wentworth would be married. They would return to Uppercross as husband and wife, and the silent dark rooms of the Great House would be crowded with people celebrating and the sound of church bells.

Lost in these painful thoughts, Anne was relieved to hear Lady Russell's carriage come rattling up the lane. Although she was very pleased to see her beloved friend, Anne was also embarrassed. They would have to speak of Louisa's accident, and that also meant mentioning Captain Frederick Wentworth.

'So Louisa will recover?' Lady Russell asked as they drove towards Kellynch village. 'And Captain Wentworth is there with her family, you say?'

'Yes.' Anne could not meet her friend's eye. 'I believe that he and Louisa will announce their engagement as soon as she is stronger.'

'Really?' Lady Russell said. 'I wish them well.' She said no more, but Anne could tell her friend was pleased and relieved.

'Your father has rented an elegant house in a very good part of Bath.' Lady Russell changed the subject. 'He and Elizabeth have settled down there very well, although I regret that Mrs Clay is still with them.'

Anne had to drag her thoughts away from Frederick and the Musgroves in order to appear interested. She would have been ashamed if Lady Russell had realised how much more she was thinking of Lyme than of Bath.

Anne and Lady Russell were to remain in Kellynch for a few weeks before travelling on to Bath. The first three or four days passed quietly, except for a note left at the house for Anne. The brief note said that Louisa was feeling much better, but Anne had no idea where it had come from. It was not signed.

'My dear Anne, you know for politeness we must call on Mrs Croft at Kellynch Hall,' Lady Russell said the day after the note had been left. 'Can you bear it? Are you brave enough to come with me today?'

'Of course,' Anne replied firmly, determined to do the right thing.

When Anne and Lady Russell arrived at Kellynch Hall, Mrs Croft welcomed them kindly. Anne found it easier than she thought it would be to see her former home again. The Crofts kept the large house neat and shining, and they were both such kind, pleasant people. She was relieved that Kellynch Hall was in good hands.

'This accident at Lyme is a terrible thing indeed,' Mrs Croft observed as they took tea in the drawing room. 'Poor Miss Louisa! My brother Frederick rode here from Lyme yesterday to give us the latest news.'

So that was where my note came from, Anne thought.

Mrs Croft smiled at her. 'Frederick asked after you,' she told Anne. 'He said you took control of the whole situation in a very calm, sensible manner, and he could not thank you enough.'

This gave Anne great pleasure.

'Is your brother still here?' Lady Russell asked. Anne was glad her friend had asked the question, because she wanted to hear the answer herself.

'No, he has returned to Lyme, and he declared he would not leave until Miss Louisa is well again,' Mrs Croft replied.

Then we shall hear news of their engagement some time very soon, Anne thought miserably. *Perhaps the next time I see Frederick, he will actually be married.*

'I hope Louisa does not suffer any lasting injury from her fall,' Mrs Croft remarked. 'Her behaviour was very unwise, was it not, Lady Russell?'

'Indeed,' Lady Russell agreed. 'I hope she learns to be more sensible in future.'

'It is a bad business, indeed!' exclaimed Admiral

Croft, who had just come into the drawing room to join them. 'It is a new way for a fellow to treat his girl, by breaking her head open! Is it not, Miss Elliot?'

Anne could not help smiling.

'Now, this must be very difficult for you,' Admiral Croft said, suddenly looking quite serious. 'To come here and find us in your old family home! Do feel free to go around the house, if you like.'

'I thank you, sir,' Anne replied gratefully, 'But not now.'

'You'll see that we have made very few changes,' the Admiral continued. 'I have done very little except to remove some of the mirrors in your father's bedroom. I should think Sir Walter must be a very dressy man for his time of life, Miss Anne. Such a large number of mirrors, and all for one man!'

Anne had to stop herself from laughing. Admiral Croft was a little rough and ready for Lady Russell, but he had a good heart, Anne thought. Lady Russell and Mrs Croft got along very well together, but they would not be visiting each other again for a while as the Crofts explained that they were going away for a few weeks very soon to visit some old friends. They would probably not be back at Kellynch before Lady Russell and Anne left for Bath.

However, Anne and Lady Russell had other visitors after the Crofts had left for their trip. The first of the Musgroves to return from Lyme were Charles and Mary. A few days after they'd arrived back at Uppercross, they drove over to Kellynch to see Anne and Lady Russell.

'Louisa was still quite weak when we left,' Charles informed them, 'although she was beginning to sit up.'

'We were all in lodgings together nearby,' Mary added, 'and Mrs Musgrove looked after the Harville children so the house could be kept quiet for Louisa.'

'I am so glad to hear Louisa is improving,' Anne said, very sincerely.

'She is a lucky girl,' Lady Russell observed. 'It might have been so much worse.'

'The Harvilles have been wonderful throughout this whole sad business,' Charles continued. 'Especially Mrs Harville. Nothing has been too much trouble for her.'

'Mrs Harville has had plenty of help from *me*,' Mary interrupted her husband. 'Goodness me, there was so much going on every day, I hardly had any time to myself! We had lots of lovely walks around the harbour, and I borrowed books from the library. We went to church, of course, and there were so many new people to look at, more than at Uppercross. Oh, and we visited Charmouth too, and bathed in the sea. I was just glad I could be so very useful to Louisa!'

'My parents were hoping to bring Louisa home to Uppercross for Christmas, but the doctor says it is too soon for her to be moved.' Charles sighed deeply. 'And Captain Wentworth has left Lyme. He felt that Louisa needed time and space to recover.'

Anne was surprised by this. Not long ago, Mrs Croft had told them that Captain Wentworth had intended to stay in Lyme. However, she had no doubt that Frederick would return as soon as Louisa was better.

'Anne, you must have told Lady Russell that we saw Mr William Elliot at Lyme?' Mary turned to her sister eagerly. 'It was extraordinary that we just missed speaking to each other! He looked like the perfect gentleman.'

'Mr William Elliot is a man whom I have no wish to see, Mary.' Lady Russell shook her head sternly. 'His rudeness to your father cannot be forgiven.'

Mary was silenced.

'And how is Captain Benwick?' asked Anne, changing the subject. She smiled as she remembered her walks with the young man.

Mary frowned. 'Oh, Captain Benwick is very well, I believe. But he is a strange man! We invited him to come to Uppercross to stay with us for a few days, and he seemed delighted. But then the night before we left Lyme he made a very awkward excuse and said that he'd never meant to come and stay, and that we had misunderstood. How rude!'

Charles was laughing. 'Now, Mary, you know very well how it really was! Benwick thought that *you* lived at Uppercross, my dear Anne. Then he discovered that you did not, and his courage failed him!' He smiled at Anne. 'He spoke of you one time, and said you were all "elegance, sweetness and beauty". Those were his exact words.'

'I am flattered,' Anne replied with a smile.

'Benwick might very well turn up here at Lady Russell's house to visit you,' Charles told her.

'I look forward to meeting him,' Lady Russell said with interest.

From this time on, both Anne and Lady Russell were thinking of Captain James Benwick. Every time a visitor was announced, they wondered if it might be him. But when he did not appear after a week, Lady Russell gave up on him. Anne was a little disappointed, but her thoughts soon turned another way when she received a letter from her sister Elizabeth.

Mr William Elliot is in Bath, Elizabeth wrote, *And what is more, he has visited us in our new house three times already! Our father believes that Mr Elliot wishes to forget the past and be accepted as part of our family again.*

Anne was very surprised by this and was quick to inform Lady Russell. Although Lady Russell had told Mary she didn't wish to meet Mr Elliot, she immediately changed her mind. Now she wanted to discover if he really was as eager to make things up with his family as Elizabeth claimed.

Anne was not as interested or as curious as her

friend. But she felt that she would rather see Mr Elliot again than not, which was more than she could say for many other people in Bath! Either way, she would see them all very soon.

CHAPTER TWELVE

On a dark, rainy, miserable afternoon, Anne and Lady Russell left for Bath. Anne tried not to feel too depressed as the carriage at last pulled to a halt outside her father's new home in Camden Place and her luggage was unpacked. It was an elegant house with columns on each side of the entrance, but it was not Kellynch Hall. As Lady Russell drove off to her own lodgings, Anne entered the house with a sinking heart. She wondered how many months she would be living here, and how long it would be before she heard of Frederick's marriage to Louisa.

Oh, when shall I leave here again? she thought sadly, untying her damp bonnet.

'Anne, you are here at last!' Elizabeth exclaimed as she, Sir Walter and Mrs Clay came to greet her. Anne was a little startled by the warmth of their welcome, but was cheered by it all the same. Her father and sister were in excellent spirits. Anne soon realised they were mostly pleased to see her so that they could show her around the house and tell her all about their life in Bath. They were not at all interested in what had happened in Uppercross or Kellynch.

'Our house is the best in Camden Place, I assure you,' Elizabeth boasted as she led Anne into the charming drawing room. The sofas were yellow silk, and the wallpaper was patterned with exotic birds. 'Everyone here wants to know us.'

'We have visitors calling every day,' Sir Walter observed with satisfaction. 'We turn down many invitations to dine, but still people send them!'

Anne sighed very softly as Elizabeth threw open a set of folding doors and proudly displayed the red and gold dining room. It was a fine house, to be sure, but it was not Kellynch Hall. Did her father and sister not miss their old home at all?

It wasn't long before Sir Walter and Elizabeth began to speak of Mr William Elliot. They had a great deal to tell Anne about Mr Elliot.

'He has been in Bath for two weeks,' her father told Anne. 'He came to call on us as soon as he arrived.'

'He has apologised so nicely!' Elizabeth declared, with a joyful smile. 'He explained that he had *never* been disrespectful about either me or my father. He said that someone had been telling lies about him.'

'Certainly, Mr Elliot's marriage to that low-born woman was a terrible thing,' said Sir Walter. 'But now he is a widower, he is free to marry again.' Anne noticed Elizabeth blush a little.

As Sir Walter and Elizabeth talked on, Anne really did not know what to think. Why should Mr William Elliot be so keen to make things up with Sir Walter? It seemed strange to Anne. Mr Elliot had nothing to gain by doing so. He was undoubtedly the richer man of the two, and he would be Sir William and inherit Kellynch Hall when Anne's father died. It must be, Anne decided, because Mr Elliot was interested in taking Elizabeth as his second wife.

'Mr Elliot has dined with us once already, and will come again very soon,' Elizabeth told her sister. And the glance that passed between Elizabeth and Mrs Clay told Anne they both believed that Mr Elliot was visiting to see Elizabeth.

'I saw Mr William Elliot at Lyme—' Anne began, but her father interrupted her, without waiting to hear any details.

'Then you would have noticed his very gentleman-like appearance. He has an air of elegance and good sense. However' – Sir Walter frowned – 'he has a very weak chin. And he has aged since the last time we saw him. Mr Elliot said that I looked exactly the same as I did when we met before, all those years ago. But I could not say the same about *him,* which embarrassed me.'

During dinner, the whole conversation was about Mr Elliot and his good friend Colonel Wallis, who was staying in Bath. Colonel Wallis had been invited to dinner with the Elliots too. His wife had remained at home as she was about to have a baby, and so they had not met her yet.

'Mrs Wallis is said to be a beautiful woman,' Sir Walter remarked as they ate their beef and potatoes. 'I long to see her. It will make up for all the very plain women that I see every day on the streets of Bath!'

As they left the table and went to the drawing room, there was a knock at the door.

'Who *can* this be?' Elizabeth asked. 'It is quite late.' Her eyes began to sparkle with excitement. 'Could it be Mr Elliot?'

'He said he was dining in Lansdown Crescent tonight,' Sir Walter remembered. 'That is only a few streets away. Perhaps he is calling in on us on his way home.'

'I believe it is Mr Elliot's knock,' Mrs Clay said eagerly, glancing at Elizabeth, who looked gleeful.

And indeed it *was* Mr William Elliot, the very

same man Anne had seen twice in Lyme. She drew back a little as he greeted the others, and waited until Sir Walter said, 'Allow me to present my daughter, Anne.'

Anne stepped forward, smiling and blushing, and Mr Elliot gave a little start of surprise. He had recognised her immediately.

'Are we not friends already?' he asked in a very easy manner as he bowed over her hand. 'Although I had no idea who you were when I met you in Lyme!'

'Nor I you,' Anne replied. 'You were leaving Lyme before we discovered who you were.'

Mr Elliot sat down with them in the drawing room, and Anne soon realised that her first impressions of him were correct. He was sensible and good-tempered, and an interesting person to talk to – the complete gentleman.

'Pray tell me your business in Lyme, and your impressions of the place?' Mr Elliot said, turning to Anne as soon as there was a pause in the conversation.

'We were there for pleasure,' Anne replied. 'And I thought it was beautiful.'

'Was it not strange that we were in the same inn at exactly the same time?' Mr Elliot smiled eagerly at her. 'I was alone, but I could hear you and your friends enjoying yourselves at dinner.

If only I had asked who you were! The name "Musgrove" would have told me enough, and I could have come and joined you.'

Sir Walter claimed his attention then, with a question about Colonel and Mrs Wallis. Mr Elliot was forced to break off his conversation with Anne and talk with the others. But every so often, whenever he could, he turned back to Anne to talk of Lyme. They spoke of the wonderful walks along the Cobb, but when Anne mentioned 'an accident', Mr Elliot wanted to know the whole story. Sir Walter and Elizabeth began to question Anne also, but she knew they were only asking because Mr Elliot was interested.

'What a terrible time you have had, to be sure!' he declared. 'It must have been very worrying for you all. I wish the young lady a speedy recovery.'

Anne was comforted by Mr Elliot's concern. He stayed with them for an hour, and only began to talk of leaving when the gilt clock on the mantelpiece struck eleven. As they said their goodbyes, Anne could not have believed that her first evening in Bath could have passed so well.

CHAPTER THIRTEEN

Anne did not know if Mr William Elliot was in love with her sister Elizabeth. But she *did* want to be sure that her father had not fallen in love with Mrs Clay. When she went down to breakfast the following morning, she heard a snatch of conversation between the three of them that made her very uneasy.

'Now Miss Anne is come, I suppose I am not wanted at all,' Penelope Clay was saying. And to this Elizabeth replied, 'No, no, that is not true at all. She is nothing to me, compared to you.'

'My dear madam, this must not be,' Sir Walter added as Anne entered the breakfast room. 'You must not run away from us now. You must stay and meet the beautiful Mrs Wallis. Indeed you must.'

Sir Walter spoke so firmly that Anne was not surprised to see Mrs Clay steal a nervous glance at Elizabeth and herself.

Later that morning, Anne and her father happened to be alone together, and he began to remark on her looks.

'You seem less thin, my dear Anne. Your skin, your complexion, is greatly improved. It is clearer and fresher. Have you been using Gowland's Lotion?'

'No, nothing,' Anne replied.

'You are looking very well,' her father said with approval. 'But if you were not, I would recommend using that lotion every day. I suggested it to Mrs Clay, and you can see how much her skin has improved!'

Anne was startled. Mrs Clay looked exactly the same to her as when she'd left Kellynch Hall! *Never mind, things must take their course*, Anne thought with a sigh. There was nothing she could do about it. And if Sir Walter *did* decide to marry Penelope Clay, Anne could always find a loving home with Lady Russell.

Lady Russell was enjoying herself very much in Bath. The sight of Mrs Clay in so much favour and of Anne being ignored annoyed her, but she was eager to meet Mr Elliot when she was invited to dinner at Camden Place.

'*Can* this be Mr Elliot?' Lady Russell marvelled when she discussed him later with Anne later once they were alone. 'What an agreeable man he is! Do you not think the same, Anne?

'Yes,' Anne replied, but she was a little hesitant. 'I do not understand, though, why he is so keen to be part of the family again after all this time apart. Does that not seem strange to you?'

'I think it is very natural,' Lady Russell replied thoughtfully. 'Now he is older, he sees the value of being on good terms with his relatives.'

'Or perhaps Elizabeth is his object,' Anne suggested.

'Elizabeth?' Lady Russell smiled. 'Very well. Time will tell.'

Anne realised what Lady Russell was implying, but could not believe that Mr Elliot would prefer herself to Elizabeth. And she was not interested in him that way, either. Although Mr Elliot *seemed* very much the gentleman, she still knew very little about him. However, he was the most interesting person she had met in Bath so far, and she enjoyed talking to him. That was enough for the moment.

She did wish, though, that her father and Elizabeth could be more dignified. Sir Walter had read in the Bath newspaper that his cousin, Lady Dalrymple, and her daughter were in town. So now Sir Walter and Elizabeth were in a flutter of anxiety. The two families had lost touch years before, as a result of a falling-out, but Sir Walter and Elizabeth desperately wished to make up. It would be something to boast about, that they were related to such an important person as Lady Dalrymple! But how could they open contact with her again, after all these years?

Anne was soon very bored with hearing the name 'Dalrymple', as her father and sister could talk of nothing else.

'I have written to Lady Dalrymple to apologise for our disagreement, and have requested that we may visit her,' Sir Walter announced to Elizabeth a few days later. To their delight, Lady Dalrymple graciously accepted the apology, and the two families were on speaking terms once more.

Anne was very embarrassed. Her father and sister made sure that everyone knew about their high-born relatives, and talked about them constantly. But Lady Dalrymple and her daughter were not particularly special. They were quite ordinary. They were not interesting, and they were not lively company. Also, Lady Dalrymple's daughter was so plain and awkward that Anne knew Sir Walter would have remarked on it, if it had been anybody else.

'Do you think the Dalrymples are worth all this effort?' Anne asked Mr Elliot one evening when they were in the drawing room at Camden Place. He had escorted them home through the lamp-lit streets after they'd had dinner at the Dalrymples' splendid house. 'Just because they are rich and important people?'

'My dear Anne, I know what you are saying,' Mr Elliot replied. 'But remember they are part of our family. Perhaps they themselves are not the best company, but they will gather interesting people around them. And we all will benefit from that.' He paused suddenly, his expression serious, and lowered his voice. 'I am sure we both feel that *any* company that distracts your father is a very good thing.' As he spoke, Mr Elliot glanced at the empty chair where Mrs Clay had very recently been sitting. Anne perfectly understood his meaning. So Mr Elliot had noticed something going on between Mrs Clay and Sir Walter too!

While Sir Walter and Elizabeth were enjoying calling on the Dalrymples every day, Anne was seeking out a friend of her own. She had heard that a former schoolfriend of hers was in Bath. Mrs Smith had lost her husband, and had fallen on hard times, so Anne was determined to visit her.

'My very dear Anne!' Mrs Smith's pale, worn face lit up instantly when Anne was shown into her rooms at the boarding house. 'How glad I am to see you after all these years!'

'And I am so happy to be here!' Anne pressed her old friend's hand affectionately, although she was troubled. Mrs Smith was clearly quite ill, and the boarding house that was her home was dark and shabby, although very clean. Anne was surprised, as she'd heard that her friend had married a rich man.

'How well you look!' Mrs Smith exclaimed as Anne seated herself. 'Excuse me for not rising from my chair, but the pain in my legs is so very bad. I cannot stand without help.'

They began to talk, a little awkwardly at first as they hadn't seen each other for many years.

But after a few minutes, they were chatting away like the old, dear friends they were.

Anne was astonished and upset by the story of her friend's life since their schooldays. Mrs Smith's husband had died of a serious illness, having spent every penny of their money. She had no children and was all alone with no home except the boarding house.

And yet Anne was impressed by her friend's good humour, her interest in other people and the way she found something to be grateful for every day.

'My landlady Mrs Speed is very kind to me,' Mrs Smith confided in Anne. 'Her sister is a nurse, and she has been looking after me when she is not working. Isn't that kind of her? I love to hear Nurse Rooke tell me all about her patients! At the moment she is caring for Mrs Wallis, the wife of a Colonel Wallis. She is about to have a baby, and is a very pretty woman, I believe!'

Anne realised that she was talking about Mr Elliot's friends and was about to say so, but Mrs Smith began to speak of something else.

It was some time before Sir Walter and Elizabeth discovered that Anne had been regularly visiting Mrs Smith. They had all been invited to spend the evening with Lady Dalrymple, including Lady Russell, but Anne had refused.

'I am visiting an old schoolfriend tonight, so I cannot come,' Anne explained. 'Lady Russell is happy to send her carriage to take me there, as she has done before.'

'And who is this schoolfriend?' Sir Walter asked. When Anne told him about Mrs Smith, her father pulled a face.

'Mrs Smith?' he repeated with a sneer. 'A poor widow living in a poor part of town? This is the chosen friend of Miss Anne Elliot, and she wishes to spend time with her, instead of with her own relatives? Mrs Smith, indeed!'

Anne would not change her mind, however. She went to see Mrs Smith, as she had arranged, and the next day, Lady Russell told her all about the evening at Lady Dalrymple's.

'Mr Elliot asked *very* particularly where you were,' Lady Russell said with a smile. 'I explained to him about Mrs Smith, and he was delighted with your kindness. Mr Elliot is becoming very fond of you, my dear.'

Anne blushed at her friend's meaning and gently shook her head.

'I think the two of you could be very happy together,' Lady Russell insisted. 'And in time, I would be so delighted to see you take your mother's old place, as mistress of Kellynch Hall!'

Anne's heart swelled with emotion as she pictured herself as Lady Elliot of Kellynch Hall, the wife of Mr William Elliot. But the thought only lasted for a few seconds. Much as she liked Mr Elliot, she was still not sure he was everything he appeared to be. His past behaviour to her father and her sister had been appalling, even though it was many years ago. Besides, there was only one man for her . . .

Anne was now becoming very anxious to hear the latest news from Uppercross and from Lyme. It had been three weeks since Mary's last letter. Anne did not know if Louisa was still at Lyme, or if Frederick had returned there. She was thinking about them all during breakfast the following morning, when the maid came into the room.

'A letter for you, madam,' the maid said, handing it to Anne. 'With the good wishes of Admiral and Mrs Croft.'

'The Crofts who rent Kellynch?' Sir Walter exclaimed. 'So, they are in Bath. Who is the letter from, Anne?'

'It is from Mary,' Anne replied before escaping to her bedroom. She tore the letter open, trembling with fear as she did so. Would it contain news of Louisa's engagement to Frederick Wentworth?

The letter was a very long one, which increased Anne's fears. The first part was, as usual, full of complaints.

We have had terrible weather here, and a very dull Christmas, Mary wrote. *No one has come calling on us at all. However, today the carriage goes to Lyme to collect Louisa at last. The Harvilles are coming with her to stay at the Great House.*

We have just heard that the Crofts are leaving for Bath. I am quite disgusted that they have not asked me if they can take anything like a letter or a parcel to you. What bad neighbours they are!

This was scribbled on the first sheet of paper,

and Anne turned impatiently to the second page.

I did not finish my letter on purpose so that I could wait and tell you how Louisa is, now she is home, Mary continued. *And I also had a very friendly note from Mrs Croft, asking if I had anything I wished her to bring to Bath for you. What pleasant neighbours they are!*

But now for Louisa. She and the Harvilles arrived at the Great House yesterday. Charles and I went to see her, of course. And we discovered that Louisa is to marry Captain Benwick!

Are you not very surprised, Anne?

CHAPTER FOURTEEN

Anne was more than surprised. She was thunderstruck. Her legs would not support her, and she sank down on to her bed. She read and reread the same sentence again and again. *Louisa is to marry Captain Benwick!* The words danced up and down on the page before her eyes. How was this possible? It was almost too wonderful to believe! But what did Frederick think of it all?

Anne simply could not understand it. Lively, laughing, chattering Louisa and quiet, thoughtful, poetry-loving Captain Benwick! How had this happened?

It must be because they spent so much time together

while Louisa was recovering, Anne thought, reading Mary's letter through yet again.

She saw no reason for the couple not to be happy together. Captain Benwick would become more cheerful, and his quiet, steady manner would calm Louisa down a little. As long as Frederick was not unhappy about it, then this unexpected turn of events was nothing to worry about. Anne's eyes sparkled with happiness at the thought of Frederick as a free man!

Anne was now very eager to meet with the Crofts to find out how Frederick had taken the news of Louisa's engagement to Benwick. But when the Crofts visited the Elliots a few days later, they did not mention it, and Anne guessed they had not heard yet. It would not be long before they did, though.

About a week later, Anne was walking through the muddy streets of Bath towards Camden Place when she spotted Admiral Croft. He was standing outside a picture gallery, staring intently at a painting in the window. He did not notice Anne approaching and she had to tap his arm gently to get his attention.

'Ah, Miss Anne, is it you?' Admiral Croft beamed at her. 'I did not see you. This picture has made me

smile!' Anne saw that the painting in the window was of a ship sailing on the high seas. 'I wonder where that boat was built,' the Admiral chuckled. 'I would not sail across a pond in it! Now' – he turned to Anne and held out his arm – 'where are you going? May I escort you somewhere?'

'I am going home,' Anne replied, taking his arm.

'And I think your lodgings are the same way, so shall we walk together a little?'

'I should like it very much,' the Admiral agreed. 'And I have something to tell you, too, my dear.' Anne's heart beat harder. Surely the Admiral and Mrs Croft must have heard about Louisa's engagement to Captain Benwick by now? And they must have heard about it from Frederick himself.

'Dear me, what a ship that is!' the Admiral remarked as they left the picture gallery behind them and walked on. Then he halted, spotting somebody he recognised. 'Let me stop but a moment to say hello to a friend of mine, Captain Brigden. Here he is, coming towards us.'

Anne waited as patiently as she could while the Admiral greeted his friend. But as they set off again, she could not help asking, 'Did you say you had something to tell me, sir?'

'Well, now, you shall hear something that will

surprise you,' he said at last. 'It is about the Miss Musgrove that all this has been happening to. I forget her name.'

'Louisa?' Anne suggested quickly.

'Yes, Louisa, that's the name. Well, we all thought she was to marry Frederick. Sophy and I wondered what they were waiting for. Then after the accident, it was clear that they *must* wait, until she had recovered. Frederick told us he would stay in Lyme, but then very shortly afterwards he left for Shropshire to stay with his brother Edward!' Admiral Croft looked bemused. 'And there he has been ever since. Even my wife could not understand it. Not only that, but now Miss Louisa is to marry Captain James Benwick!' The Admiral shook his head in disbelief. 'Do you know Captain Benwick?'

'A little. He is a very pleasant young man.'

'Oh, yes, you ladies are the best judge. But Sophy and I were shocked. We had a letter from Frederick yesterday telling us all about it.'

'I hope Captain Wentworth is not too upset?' Anne asked anxiously, longing to know how Frederick was feeling.

'Not at all. There is not a curse in the letter from beginning to end.'

Anne looked down to hide a smile.

'No, Frederick is not that kind of man. If the girl likes Captain Benwick better, it is quite right that she should marry *him*.'

'Certainly,' Anne replied. 'But I hope Captain Wentworth does not feel ill-used by Captain Benwick. I would hate to see their close friendship destroyed by this.'

'Yes, yes, I understand you. But there is no hint of this in Frederick's letter. He hopes they will be very happy together, and that is all.'

'I am glad to hear it,' Anne said, hoping it was true.

'Poor Frederick!' Admiral Croft sighed. 'Now he must begin all over again with someone else.

My wife plans to write and tell him to come and stay with us here. Do you not think, Miss Anne, that we should get Frederick to come to Bath?'

Anne was too flustered to reply and managed to turn the conversation. But she did not know that while she was walking with Admiral Croft, Captain Wentworth was in fact already on his way to Bath. And the very next time Anne went out, she saw him.

Anne had been shopping with Elizabeth and Mrs Clay, escorted by Mr William Elliot. They had been to almost all the fashionable shops in Bath when suddenly it began to rain. Only Mr Elliot had an umbrella, so they quickly took shelter in Molland's, a popular bakery.

'I believe that it is Lady Dalrymple's carriage across the street,' Mr Elliot said, peering out of the window. 'Let me run over and ask if she could take you ladies home.'

Mr Elliot soon returned with the news that Lady Dalrymple would be happy to take them home. She still had some shopping to do and would call for them in ten minutes' time. However, Lady Dalrymple had her daughter with her so there was only room for two more ladies in her carriage. Anne immediately said that she would be happy to walk home with Mr Elliot. While they waited for Lady Dalrymple, Mr Elliot kindly took it upon himself to run a final errand for Mrs Clay so that she didn't have to go out in the rain. When he returned, he would escort Anne home.

It was just after Mr Elliot had gone that Anne got the shock of her life. Captain Frederick Wentworth himself was walking down the street towards Molland's! Anne was so surprised, she half-rose from her chair, then sank down again in confusion. He was with a party of ladies and gentlemen whom Anne did not recognise. They turned into Molland's doorway, and the next moment Frederick came face to face with Anne. She, at least, was prepared, having already seen him, but Frederick was not. He turned chalk-white, and then very red.

'Miss Elliot – Anne!' he exclaimed. Anne thought he looked embarrassed and uncomfortable. But what did this behaviour of his mean? What were his feelings towards her? Anne could not tell.

Frederick was composing himself now. 'You are well?' he asked her quietly.

'Very well, I thank you,' Anne replied. She saw Elizabeth glance at them. Her sister had recognised Captain Wentworth but refused to speak to him or even nod at him. Elizabeth simply turned away coldly, which caused Anne great pain.

At that moment Lady Dalrymple's carriage drew up outside Molland's.

'Ah, here is my cousin Lady Dalrymple, just as she promised,' Elizabeth announced loudly, so that everyone in the bakery could hear her. 'Come, Penelope.'

'Do you not go too?' Frederick asked as Elizabeth and Mrs Clay hurried outside.

'There is not enough room in the carriage,' Anne replied. 'I shall walk home.'

'But it rains!'

'Oh, only a little.'

'May I offer you my umbrella?' Frederick said kindly, holding it out with a smile.

'Thank you, but I am just waiting for Mr Elliot,

and he has an umbrella,' Anne replied gently. 'I am sure he will be here in a moment.'

She had hardly finished speaking when Mr Elliot arrived.

'My dear Anne,' he cried, 'I am so sorry to keep you waiting! Shall we go?'

'Good morning to you,' Anne said softly to Frederick, taking Mr Elliot's arm. They walked away together, Mr Elliot holding the umbrella above them both.

If Anne had looked back, she would have seen Frederick at the window, staring after her and Mr Elliot as they made their way along the street.

CHAPTER FIFTEEN

Anne could not concentrate on what Mr Elliot was saying as they walked back to Camden Place. She could only think about Frederick. She longed to understand his feelings, and whether he was disappointed about losing Louisa Musgrove to his friend or not. Anne still wasn't sure.

And when would she see him again? She had no idea, but they were bound to meet at one of the fashionable parties in town. Anne had also realised that she would have to tell Lady Russell that Frederick was not to marry Louisa, and was still a free man.

'Louisa is to marry Captain *Benwick*?' Lady Russell exclaimed when Anne summoned up the courage to break the news to her the following day. 'How very unexpected!' Anne could tell that her friend was surprised and concerned. She knew very well that Lady Russell favoured Mr Elliot and hoped that there would soon be a proposal of marriage for Anne. Lady Russell obviously did not want Captain Frederick Wentworth in the picture at all.

Another day or two passed, but Anne did not see Frederick again. However, the Elliots and Lady Russell were to go to an evening concert arranged by Lady Dalrymple. The music would be very good, and Anne was sure that Frederick would attend. She was impatient to see him again. Anne had half-promised to spend that evening with her friend Mrs Smith, but she visited her briefly to put it off.

'We are all to go to the concert tonight,' Anne told her friend. 'Lady Russell and Mr Elliot are coming with us. I shall call on you again tomorrow, and it will be a much longer visit, I promise you.'

'I shall look forward to it,' Mrs Smith replied with a twinkle in her eyes, 'for I begin to feel sure that I will not have many more visits from you!'

Anne was startled and a little confused, but did not have time to ask what her friend meant. She had to hurry home and get ready for the concert.

Sir Walter, his two daughters and Mrs Clay were first to arrive at the elegant Octagon Room where the concert was to take place that evening. Anne wore her new rose-pink silk gown, and as she settled herself by the fire, she wondered if was right in thinking that Frederick would come.

A few moments later, the door opened and Captain Wentworth walked in, quite alone. Anne blushed as rose-pink as her dress, but immediately said, 'How do you do?'

Frederick hesitated, then came to stand near her. They talked a little awkwardly of the Bath weather for a minute or two, but Anne was conscious of Sir Walter and Elizabeth in the background. They were whispering together.

Then Captain Wentworth bowed slightly in their direction. Anne realised that meant her father and Elizabeth had decided to greet him, however coldly. This raised her spirits a good deal.

'I have hardly seen you since Lyme,' Frederick said with a smile. 'It was a terrible day, but at least there is now happiness to follow. When you suggested Benwick fetch the doctor, you could not have known he would be so important to Louisa's recovery!'

'No, I could not.' Anne returned the smile. 'But I hope it will be a good match. They are both such pleasant people.'

'Yes,' Captain Wentworth agreed rather hesitantly. 'But I do think there is a great difference between them. Louisa is a sweet girl, but Benwick is something more. He is thoughtful and intelligent, a man of learning. He was very much in love with Frances Harville before she died, and she, too, was a very clever and well-educated woman. He and Frances were much better matched, and Benwick was devoted to her. A man does not recover so quickly from such a strong first love. He does *not*!'

Anne could hardly breathe. The room suddenly seemed hot and stuffy, with too many people now coming in every moment, the door slamming behind them. Suddenly the name of Lady Dalrymple was announced, and Sir Walter and Elizabeth quickly stepped forward to greet their important relative. Lady Dalrymple and her daughter were escorted by Mr Elliot and his friend Colonel Wallis, and Anne became separated from Captain Wentworth, who went to another part of the room. Anne longed to speak more with him. In the last ten minutes she had learnt more about his feelings for Louisa Musgrove than she'd dared hope for.

Anne's eyes sparkled and her cheeks glowed as they all settled themselves to listen to the opening music, played on a harp. As the lilting sounds

echoed around the room, Anne thought over what Frederick had just said – his look, his embarrassment, his words about the power of a first love. Could it be that his heart had returned to her? The thought thrilled her beyond anything.

Anne glanced around the concert room but could not catch Frederick's eye. It did not matter. There would be time enough.

During the first half of the concert, after a song sung in Italian, Anne found herself attempting to translate the words of the song for Mr Elliot. They held a concert programme between them, their heads bent close together.

'I think this is the meaning of it,' Anne told him, 'but I am certainly not a clever Italian student!'

'Yes, yes, I see that,' Mr Elliot replied, smiling. 'Your translation is clear, simple and elegant. I see you are a very poor student indeed!'

Anne laughed. 'You are too kind.'

'And you are too modest, Anne. However, I

know what an intelligent, talented woman you are,' Mr Elliot continued. 'I have been hearing reports about you for many years, long before we met here in Bath.'

Anne was surprised. 'From whom, pray?'

'That I cannot say,' Mr Elliot replied mysteriously. 'But I found out a great deal about you. The name of "Anne Elliot" has charmed me for a very long time.' He lowered his voice. 'And if I dared, I would wish that your name would never change.'

It was almost a proposal of marriage, but Anne was no longer paying much attention to Mr Elliot. Instead her attention had been caught by her father and Lady Dalrymple discussing Captain Wentworth.

'He is a fine-looking young man indeed!' Lady Dalrymple was saying approvingly.

'Yes,' Sir Walter agreed. 'A very handsome man. His sister and her husband rent Kellynch Hall.'

Anne turned her head and caught Frederick's

eye, but he instantly looked away. Anne was a little upset, and began to wish Mr Elliot was not sitting so close to her.

When the first part of the concert was over, people began leaving to take tea during the interval. Anne remained in her seat, hoping Frederick would come to speak to her. But he did not. Then, when everyone returned for the second half, there was a change in their seating arrangements. Elizabeth invited Mr Elliot to sit between herself and Lady Dalrymple's daughter, and Colonel Wallis went to sit with some other friends. So Anne was able to change seats and move to the end of the row, where she might more easily speak to Frederick if he passed by.

Before the music started again, Frederick appeared. He came towards Anne slowly, looking very serious, which puzzled her.

'I am disappointed,' Frederick told her gravely. 'The music is not as good as I was expecting. I will not be sorry when the concert is over.'

'But the harpist was very talented, was she not?' asked Anne with a gentle smile. They talked a little more, and Frederick seemed to cheer up. He glanced down at the empty seat next to Anne as if he intended to sit there.

Then Anne felt a tap on her shoulder. It was Mr Elliot, asking Anne to translate the next song, which was again in Italian. Lady Dalrymple's daughter was anxious to know the meaning of it. Anne could not refuse, but she dealt with the request as quickly as possible before turning back to Frederick. To her dismay, he looked stern and serious again.

'I must wish you good night,' he said abruptly. 'I am going home.'

'Is this song not worth staying for?' Anne asked.

'No,' Frederick replied. 'There is nothing worth my staying for.' And then he was gone.

And that was when a thought struck Anne

– could it be that Frederick was jealous of Mr Elliot? She could hardly believe it. It was something she could never have imagined after their first meeting at Uppercross all those weeks ago. For a moment, she was delighted, but this feeling did not last long. She *must* let Frederick know the truth, that Mr Elliot was nothing to her except a relative she was fond of. But how was that to be done?

CHAPTER SIXTEEN

Anne was pleased she had arranged to see Mrs Smith the next day. She would be out when Mr Elliot called, and she meant to avoid him at all costs. She had no bad feelings towards Mr Elliot, however. If there had been no such person as Frederick Wentworth, then perhaps she *might* have returned Mr Elliot's affection. But whatever happened between herself and Frederick now, there was no other man for her.

Mrs Smith was eager to hear all about the concert and questioned Anne about the evening as soon as she arrived. 'Who was there?' she asked. 'The Durand family? Old Lady Maclean? The Ibbotsons?'

'I do not know,' Anne confessed. 'I should have taken more notice.'

'But you had a pleasant evening!' Mrs Smith exclaimed. 'I see it in your eyes. You were in company last night with the person you care most about in the world!'

Anne was very embarrassed and could say nothing.

'Pray, does Mr Elliot know that I am in Bath?' Mrs Smith asked very unexpectedly. Anne stared at her in surprise.

'Mr Elliot?' she repeated. 'Do you know Mr Elliot?'

'I did,' Mrs Smith replied gravely. 'But no longer, it seems. It is a great while since we last met.'

Anne was amazed. She had had no idea.

'Mr Elliot is in a position to do me a great favour,' Mrs Smith added. 'I would be grateful if you could speak to him on my behalf, now that you and he are so close.'

'Mr Elliot and I are only friends,' Anne said, puzzled. Mrs Smith frowned.

'I see that it has not been officially announced yet, then,' she said thoughtfully. 'But you do not intend to keep him waiting, I hope? Please do not forget me when you are married!'

'You are mistaken, indeed you are,' Anne cried earnestly. 'I have great respect for Mr Elliot, but I am not going to marry him. I have not known him long, and I still have some concerns about his past behaviour. No, it was *not* Mr Elliot whom I was so happy to meet at the concert last night . . .'

Anne stopped abruptly, wishing she had not said so much.

'Very well.' Mrs Smith finally looked convinced of the truth.

'But why would you think I was planning to marry Mr Elliot?' Anne asked, mystified.

'I only heard of it two days ago,' Mrs Smith

replied. 'Did you notice the woman who opened the door to you just now?'

Anne shook her head.

'It was my landlady's sister, Nurse Rooke. She was told the whole story by Mrs Wallis, the wife of Colonel Wallis, Mr Elliot's good friend.'

'The whole story!' Anne laughed. 'There is hardly anything to tell. Shall I bring Mr Elliot to visit you? I am sure he would like to come.'

Mrs Smith thought for a moment. 'No, I thank you,' she said at last.

Anne was curious. 'You must have known Mr Elliot for many years? What was he like as a very young man?'

There was silence for a few moments. Mrs Smith seemed to be unsure whether to answer Anne's question or not.

'My dear Anne,' she said at last in her normal, friendly tone. 'I do not want to make mischief, and I have not been certain what I should do for the best. But now I shall tell you. Mr William Elliot is a man without heart or conscience! He is selfish and cruel and has no feelings for others. He thinks only of himself. Oh, his heart is hollow!'

Anne was so astonished, she could not speak.

'Forgive me,' Mrs Smith went on, 'but Mr Elliot has helped to ruin my life. He was a great friend of my dear, dead husband. We were all friends, but Mr Elliot was very poor back then. He often stayed with us, and I know my husband gave him money on many occasions.'

'This must be about the time Mr Elliot first met my father and sister,' Anne said thoughtfully, 'before he married his first wife.'

'He was determined to make his fortune by marriage,' Mrs Smith told her. 'That was why he drew back from Sir Walter and Elizabeth. He did not want to marry your sister. No, he wanted a much richer wife.'

Anne remembered what Mr Elliot had said the night before. 'Did you talk about me to him?'

'Yes, I did. I used to boast of my dear friend Anne Elliot.'

'So that was how he knew about me!' Anne murmured.

'All Mr Elliot wanted back then was money,' Mrs Smith explained. 'He cared nothing for Kellynch Hall or for his family. But wait, you shall have proof.'

Mrs Smith asked Anne to go into her bedroom and bring her a small wooden box from a shelf in her wardrobe. From this, she produced a letter and gave it to Anne to read. It was from Mr Elliot to Mrs Smith's husband.

Thank you for the offer of money, but I have enough for the moment. Your kindness overwhelms me. Thank heavens, I have got rid of Sir Walter and Miss Elizabeth. They have gone back to Kellynch and made me promise to visit them. But my first visit to Kellynch will be when it is mine so I can put it up for sale. Sir Walter may marry again, though. He is fool enough to do so. I wish I had any name but Elliot, as I am sick of them all!

Anne was shocked. Mr Elliot had seemed so correct and well-mannered! It was hard to believe, even though she'd sometimes wondered if he was exactly what he appeared to be.

'This is full proof of everything you have said.' Anne handed the letter back to Mrs Smith. 'But I still do not understand why Mr Elliot wants to be friends with us *now*.'

'I can explain this too,' Mrs Smith replied with a smile. 'His attentions to your family are now very sincere because he truly wants to marry you. I heard all this from his friend, Colonel Wallis.'

'Do you know Colonel Wallis, then?'

Mrs Smith shook her head. 'No, but Colonel Wallis tells everything to his wife. And Mrs Wallis tells everything to Nurse Rooke, who is looking after her while she has her baby. Then Nurse Rooke, knowing that you are my friend, comes here and tells *me*!'

'But Mr Elliot was already visiting my father and Elizabeth before I came to Bath,' Anne pointed out. 'So that could not have been because he wanted to marry me.'

'Indeed. So now I will tell you the real reason why he befriended your father and sister. It is widely known that your sister has a friend staying with her – a sly, quiet, clever woman who is determined to marry Sir Walter.'

'Mrs Clay,' said Anne.

'Quite so. Well, it was Colonel Wallis who alerted Mr Elliot to this, and so he rushed to Bath immediately. He has since been calling on your family and keeping an eye on your sister's friend. The reason being, he cannot *bear* the idea of *not* being Sir William Elliot of Kellynch Hall. And as you know, if Mrs Clay becomes Lady Elliot and has a son, then Mr Elliot will never become Sir William.'

'I am very glad to know all this,' Anne said after a moment's thought. 'Somehow I was never satisfied that I knew Mr Elliot's true character. I am grateful to you for telling me.'

But Mrs Smith was not finished. She began

explaining to Anne how Mr Elliot had ruined her husband. After his marriage, Mr Elliot had spent his wife's great fortune freely, encouraging Mr Smith to spend alongside him. He had overspent alarmingly in an effort to keep up with Mr Elliot, and the Smiths had lost everything.

'My poor husband died just as we were made bankrupt,' Mrs Smith reported, her lips quivering with emotion. 'I applied to Mr Elliot for help, but he refused, even though my husband asked him to oversee his will. Mr Elliot simply did not care! My husband had property abroad that should now be mine, and I have written to Mr Elliot many times to ask him to claim this property for me. But he would do nothing.'

Anne expressed her sympathy. She was shuddering inwardly at the thought that she *might* have accepted Mr Elliot's proposal of marriage, if Frederick had married Louisa Musgrove. Lady Russell would have wanted it above all things. She would certainly have advised Anne to marry him. But now it was important that Lady Russell should no longer be deceived by Mr Elliot and Anne was determined to tell her the truth.

CHAPTER SEVENTEEN

The next morning, Anne decided that she must see Lady Russell and tell her what she had discovered.

'If you are going to Lady Russell, then take back this tiresome book she lent me and pretend I have read it,' Elizabeth ordered Anne. 'You need not tell her so, but I thought her dress at the concert was hideous. My best love to her, of course.'

'Say that I shall call on her soon,' Sir Walter added. 'But not in the morning. The morning light is too harsh for women of her age. If only Lady Russell would wear a little make-up!'

But before Anne could set off, a knock at the

door startled them. They were all equally surprised when Mary and Charles Musgrove appeared.

'We are staying at The White Hart inn with my mother, Captain Harville and Henrietta,' Charles explained after the greetings were over. 'Captain Harville has business here in Bath, and my mother thought it a good opportunity for Henrietta to buy her wedding clothes.'

'We left Louisa, Captain Benwick and Mrs Harville in Uppercross,' Mary added before she was taken off by Sir Walter and Elizabeth to be shown around the house.

'I hope you think Louisa perfectly recovered now?' Anne asked Charles.

'Yes,' Charles said rather hesitantly. 'But she is quieter and very different. No more running or jumping about. She sits with Benwick all day long and they read poetry together and whisper to each other!' Anne could not help smiling as Charles was called away to admire the dining room.

The visit passed well, and Elizabeth invited Charles and Mary to join them for a small party the following evening. Then Anne was persuaded by her sister and brother-in-law to go and meet with Mrs Musgrove and Henrietta. They called in on Lady Russell on the way, but Anne did not get a chance to tell her friend about Mr Elliot. *Never mind*, Anne told herself, *it can wait another day*.

When Anne, Charles and Mary reached The White Hart, Mrs Musgrove and Henrietta gave Anne the kindest welcome. They were really glad to see her again, and Anne felt warmed by their delight in her company.

'You must be with us every day, just as if we were all back at Uppercross!' Mrs Musgrove told her. Anne was only too willing, and she fell back into her old role of listening to and helping everyone. She talked with Henrietta about the most fashionable clothes shops in Bath, wrote notes for Mrs Musgrove and assisted Mary in finding her keys and unpacking her belongings. Charles, meanwhile, had gone out, but he returned half an hour later with Captain Harville and Captain Wentworth.

Anne was thrilled to see him again, but Frederick's look was still grave. He did not seem to want to be near enough for conversation and stayed on the opposite side of the room.

He still believes that I favour Mr Elliot! Anne thought, very frustrated. When *would* she get a chance to speak to Frederick and tell him the truth?

'Anne!' Mary called, her voice full of excitement. She was seated at the window, watching the passers-by. 'There is Mrs Clay, I am sure! She is deep in talk with a gentleman. Who is it?' She gasped. 'Good heavens, I recognise him now – it is Mr Elliot! You must come and look, Anne!' Mary insisted crossly. 'Now they are shaking hands. It is Mr Elliot indeed!'

To quieten Mary down, Anne moved to the window. She was astonished to see Mr Elliot walk away in one direction, Mrs Clay in the other. They were sworn enemies, so why were they meeting like this? It seemed very odd.

Anne walked away from the window, as Charles announced with a smile, 'Well, Mother, I have been to the theatre and bought tickets for tomorrow night. Am I not a good boy? I know how you love a play!'

'Tomorrow night?' Mary repeated in amazement. 'Charles, you know very well we promised to attend the party at my father's house tomorrow evening. How could you have forgotten? We are to meet Lady Dalrymple and Mr Elliot!'

Charles shrugged. 'What is Mr Elliot to me?' he asked jokingly. And Anne felt Frederick's eyes upon her, as if he was silently asking what Mr Elliot was to *her*.

'Charles, you had better change the tickets to another night,' Mrs Musgrove put in. 'Miss Anne would not be able to join us tomorrow evening, and I'm sure neither Henrietta nor I would enjoy the play without her.'

Anne loved Mrs Musgrove for her kindness. It also gave her an opportunity to say, 'I would much rather be with you all and go to the play. I take no pleasure in parties. But perhaps it would be better to change the tickets.'

Anne was very aware that Frederick was listening intently. A few moments later he walked over and stood beside her chair.

'You do not enjoy the evening parties here in Bath, then?' he asked, under cover of the noise and bustle as a parcel was delivered for Henrietta.

'Oh no! I do not play cards.'

'You were not a card-player before, I know.' Frederick paused before adding, 'But time makes many changes.'

'I am not so much changed,' Anne said, trembling with emotion.

There was silence for few moments, and then Frederick muttered, 'Eight and a half years is a long time. Such a long time!'

But before they had a chance to talk any further, Henrietta asked the ladies to accompany her to the shops, and she urged them all to leave before they had any more visitors.

Anne tried to look willing and rose from her chair, but she desperately wished for a little more conversation with Frederick. However, all Henrietta's plans were halted when the door was thrown open and the maid announced, 'Sir Walter and Miss Elliot.'

Anne's father and sister entered the room, and a hush fell over the others. There was no more laughing, talking or joking. Anne was embarrassed. The cold-hearted elegance of Sir Walter and Elizabeth had silenced everyone. They must have come to deliver the invitations for their party the following evening, Anne thought.

Anne was pleased when both her father and her sister made a point of greeting Captain Wentworth. Elizabeth even had an invitation ready for him.

'Tomorrow evening at our house in Camden Place, just a few friends,' she said with a smile, passing Frederick the card.

Anne watched him closely and could not decide whether he meant to accept the invitation or not. She could not quite believe that he would come tomorrow night, although she desperately wished he would.

Henrietta was eager to go shopping, so the ladies left the gentlemen to their own business. Anne was reluctant to go without speaking to Frederick again, but she had no choice.

Anne did not see Frederick again that day. When she finally arrived home, Elizabeth and Mrs Clay were busy making arrangements for the party the next day, and they ignored her. Anne did not care. Her thoughts were taken up with the never-ending question – would Frederick come to the party or not? Sometimes she thought he would, but then she'd change her mind.

Anne did, however, mention to Mrs Clay that

she'd seen her with Mr Elliot that morning. Mrs Clay looked very guilty, but only for a moment.

'Oh dear, yes, that is very true. I met him by chance in Bath Street.'

Anne had promised to spend all of the following day at The White Hart with the Musgroves. So after breakfast, as soon as the rain had stopped, she set off. She found that Mary and Henrietta had already gone out, but would return shortly. Mrs Croft was there, talking to Mrs Musgrove, and Captain Harville was deep in conversation with Frederick Wentworth. Anne could not prevent herself from blushing when she saw him.

Frederick was saying, 'I will write that letter about the painting now then, Harville,' and he went over to the table in the corner and took up a quill pen.

Anne became aware that Captain Harville was beckoning to her, a kindly smile on his face. She stood up and went over to him.

'Look here, Miss Elliot.' Captain Harville unwrapped the parcel he held and showed Anne what was inside. It was a small painting of a man in naval uniform. 'Do you know who this is?'

'Certainly. It is Captain Benwick.'

'Yes, and you may guess whom it is for.' Captain Harville sighed deeply. 'But it was not done for Louisa Musgrove. It was painted for my sister, Frances. But now Benwick has asked Frederick to have it reframed for his new love.' Captain Harville shook his head, looking distressed. 'Poor Frances! She would not have forgotten him so soon.'

'No woman who truly loved would forget,' Anne agreed gently.

'You think men are different?'

'I think so. I believe that we women are more constant.'

Just then Frederick's pen clattered to the floor. Anne had not realised he was quite so close to them, and she wondered if he had been trying to hear what they were saying.

'Have you finished the letter?' Captain Harville asked him.

'Five minutes more, and I shall be done,' Frederick replied.

Captain Harville turned back to Anne. 'Well, Miss Elliot, we shall never agree on this point,' he said, smiling sadly. 'If I could but make you understand how a sailor feels when he waves his last goodbye to his wife and children, not knowing if he will see them again! And then, the joy and happiness when he returns home safely and takes them in his arms once more.'

'Oh, you misunderstand me,' Anne cried. 'I know that many men have hearts as warm as women. The only difference, I think, is that women keep on loving, when all hope is gone.'

Their conversation was interrupted by Mrs Croft taking her leave. 'The Admiral and I shall see you tonight at your sister's party,' she said to Anne.

'And Frederick, you are also free tonight, are you not?'

But Frederick was folding up the letter and did not fully answer his sister. 'Yes, very true,' he murmured. 'Harville, are you ready to leave?'

'I am,' Captain Harville replied. 'Good morning, Miss Elliot.' And he and Frederick followed Mrs Croft out of the room.

Anne was upset. Not a word or a look from Frederick, and now he had gone! She stood up and walked over to the writing table where he had been sitting, to try and calm herself.

And then, suddenly, Frederick returned. 'I beg your pardon,' he told Mrs Musgrove, who was busy making a shopping list, 'I forgot my gloves.'

He crossed the room towards Anne and took his gloves from the writing table. Then, with his eyes fixed on hers, he drew a letter addressed to *Miss Anne Elliot* from beneath the scattered papers. He placed it before her with a grave look on his face and was gone again.

Anne felt the colour drain from her cheeks. Her future happiness depended on whatever was in that letter! Sinking into the chair where he had just been sitting, she unfolded the letter with hands that shook uncontrollably.

I can wait no longer. I am half agony, half hope. Tell me that I am not too late. I offer myself to you again with a heart even more your own than when you almost broke it eight and a half years ago. You must believe that men can be as constant in love as women, because I have loved none but you. For you alone I think and plan. Have you not seen this?

I must go. But a word or a look will tell me your decision, and whether I shall come to your father's house tonight.

Frederick

CHAPTER EIGHTEEN

Anne was overpowered with happiness. Such a letter was not soon to be recovered from. She was very pale, her heart still pounding and her legs shaky, when Charles, Mary and Henrietta came in.

'Anne, you look ill!' Henrietta exclaimed, rushing over to her. 'Whatever is the matter?'

'Nothing, I thank you.' Anne could hardly speak and longed to be on her own. 'However, I think I will go home.'

'But you must not walk!' Mrs Musgrove said anxiously. 'You are far too ill. We will call a carriage for you.'

'I am very well,' Anne protested. 'I do not need

a carriage.' It struck her that if she walked home, then she might meet Frederick somewhere in the streets, and she could give him his answer.

'Then go home and rest, my dear,' Mrs Musgrove told her. 'So that you are well enough for the party tonight.'

'Please do tell Captain Harville and Captain Wentworth that we are expecting them at the party.' Anne tried desperately to make sure that Frederick realised she wanted him to come. 'Will you give them the message?'

'Of course we will,' Charles assured her. 'Now, come, Anne. I shall walk you home.'

Anne really wanted to go alone, but she could not refuse her brother-in-law's kind offer.

They were walking along Union Street when quick footsteps sounded behind them. It was Frederick Wentworth. He fixed his eyes immediately on Anne's face, and she met his gaze with her own. Her radiant smile gave Frederick the answer he had been waiting for, and in an instant, his face glowed with happiness.

'Captain Wentworth, are you going as far as Camden Place?' Charles asked. 'Would you object to walking Anne home? She is a little under the weather this morning and must not be alone. And then I can just make it to my appointment.'

'Of course,' Frederick replied politely, never taking his eyes from Anne. She could see her own immense joy and excitement reflected in his face.

Charles Musgrove left them, and Anne and Frederick walked on. Their hearts were too full to speak at first, but they found a quiet, leafy spot in one of the parks, where they could at last be alone.

'I had not intended to write that letter to you today,' Frederick admitted as they strolled side by side through the flower gardens towards Camden Place. 'I believed that you were to marry Mr Elliot, and I admit I was jealous.'

'As I was of Louisa Musgrove,' Anne confessed,

almost dizzy with happiness.

'I was angry with you, and that is why I tried to replace you with Louisa,' Frederick explained ruefully. 'But I never cared for her in *that* way. However, while I waited in Lyme for her to recover, I found out that Harville and his wife considered us to be engaged! I began to wonder if her family thought this way too. I had been foolish, and now I had to pay the price. I decided that if Louisa expected us to marry, then we would marry. But I would try to weaken her interest in me by any fair means. That is why I left Lyme to visit my brother.'

'And then you heard that Louisa was to marry Captain Benwick?'

'I could not believe it! I decided to come to Bath straight away, and try for you again. I did not know if I had a chance.' Frederick took Anne's hand. 'The concert was agony for me. To see you with Mr Elliot, whom everyone thought you were going to marry. And there sitting behind you was Lady Russell, who, as you know, is no friend of *mine*!'

'I have been thinking about Lady Russell's advice to me all those years ago,' Anne said thoughtfully. 'I think I was right to be guided by her, as she stood in place of my mother. But I am not sure her advice was correct. She is such a dear friend of mine, the closest I have to a mother – do you think you can ever forgive her?'

'Not yet,' Frederick said honestly. 'But perhaps in time. Besides, I have realised that one other person may have been even more my enemy than Lady Russell.'

Anne looked puzzled.

'I am talking about myself,' Frederick explained as they walked through Camden Place. 'Tell me, if I had returned to Kellynch a few years later with my fortune made, would you have renewed our engagement?'

'Oh, yes!' Anne cried.

'It is not that I did not think of it,' Frederick sighed. 'But I was too proud. If only I had swallowed my foolish pride, then we could have been married six years ago.' He smiled warmly at Anne, and she felt her heart soar with happiness. 'But now we will never be separated again!'

The engagement of Anne Elliot and Frederick Wentworth was announced almost immediately. Sir Walter made no objection, and, in fact, he was secretly rather pleased. Captain Wentworth was a wealthy, handsome man, and therefore a worthy son-in-law. Elizabeth did nothing worse than look cold and disinterested. Mary was very pleased because her own sister had to be better than her husband's sisters, and Captain Wentworth was a much richer man than either Charles Hayter or Captain Benwick. The Crofts were delighted, and welcomed Anne warmly into their family.

Lady Russell caused Anne the most anxiety. But once she had explained Mr Elliot's true character to her friend, Lady Russell finally saw sense. She had disliked Captain Wentworth because his manners had not suited her, but then she had been deceived by Mr Elliot's politeness.

'My dearest Anne, this is almost too much to

take in all at once!' Lady Russell had exclaimed, shocked beyond belief when Anne had finished her story. 'I hardly know what to say.' She noted the pink blush in Anne's cheeks and the sparkle in her eyes. 'But you are happy?'

'So very, very happy,' Anne replied with a smile. 'And I will be even happier if you will give me your blessing.'

And so there was nothing Lady Russell could do, except forget Mr Elliot and begin to get to know Frederick Wentworth. But she was a sensible woman who loved Anne dearly, and it wasn't long before Frederick became like a son to her.

The news of Anne's engagement ruined Mr Elliot's plans most unexpectedly, and he left Bath soon after. Mrs Clay also left Bath at the same time, and when she was next heard of, she was living with Mr Elliot in London. She had given up on Sir Walter, and Anne couldn't help but wonder if Mrs Clay was now hoping to become the wife of Mr

William Elliot instead. Anne didn't care. She never wanted to see either of them ever again.

Although her new life was joyful and exciting, Anne did not forget her old friend, Mrs Smith. If it had not been for her, she might never have discovered the truth about Mr Elliot. She took Frederick to meet Mrs Smith, and he, too, was grateful to her. When Frederick discovered that Mrs Smith was trying to reclaim her husband's property abroad, he found a lawyer to act for her and helped her to sort out her husband's affairs. Soon Mrs Smith received the money that would make her life so much easier. She was Anne and Frederick's first visitor after they married, and they remained firm friends.

Anne had never expected to be so happy. Her love for Frederick, and his for her, grew stronger with each passing day. She had to learn to live alone while Frederick was away at sea, but she loved being a sailor's wife. Their story, Anne thought, was like a fairy tale, because she and Frederick would certainly live happily ever after.

Happily Ever After

A NOTE FROM NARINDER

On the face of it, Jane Austen and I have absolutely nothing in common, apart from both of us being writers. I'm an ordinary girl from an ordinary family, my dad was a bus driver and I'm mixed-race. Jane was white, and from an aristocratic family (although they didn't always have money). She was born at a time when upper-class women were expected to do very little other than look pretty and find a rich man to marry. As for going out to work, they would have fainted away at the very idea. I, on the other hand, was ambitious to make a success of my career.

So why, when I read my very first Jane Austen novel at fourteen years old, did she instantly become my favourite author? Why did I feel such a connection to Jane and her books? I think it was because she was a rebel. She did what she simply wasn't supposed to do at the time and broke all the rules – she worked as a writer, she made money for herself without needing a husband to support her, and she produced some of the best books ever written.

And this is why I love Jane Austen so much. There's always this picture in my head of a modest, well-behaved Jane taking part in the kind of activities she writes about in her books – dinners, dances, shopping trips, visiting family and friends. She sits quietly in a corner, being the model lady, but she's taking everything in, and then she goes home and writes it all down with her trademark intelligence, sly wit and clear insight into human nature. What an amazing woman!

A NOTE FROM ÉGLANTINE

My name is Églantine Ceulemans, and as you might have noticed thanks to my first name . . . I am French!

In France, we tend to associate Britain with wonderful English gardens, a unique sense of humour, William Shakespeare and, last but not least, Jane Austen!

It was such an honour to have the opportunity

to illustrate Jane Austen's stories. I have always enjoyed reading books that are filled with love, laughter and happy endings, and Austen writes all of those things brilliantly. And who wouldn't love to illustrate gorgeous dresses, stunning mansions and passionate young women standing up for their deep convictions? I also tried to do justice to Austen's humour and light-heartedness by drawing characterful people and adding in friendly pets (sometimes well-hidden and always witnessing intense but mostly funny situations!).

I discovered Jane Austen's work with Pride and Prejudice one sun-filled summer, and I have such good memories of sitting reading it in the garden beneath my grandmother's weeping willow. This setting definitely helped me to fall in love with the book, but it would be a lie to say that I wasn't moved by Elizabeth and Mr Darcy's love story and that I didn't laugh when her mother tried (with no shame at all) to marry her daughters to all the best catches in the town! I imagined all those characters in my head so vividly, and it was a real pleasure to finally illustrate them, alongside all Austen's other amazing characters.

Jane Austen is an author who managed to depict nineteenth-century England with surprising modernity. She questioned the morality of so-called well-to-do people and she managed to write smartly, sharply and independently, at time where women were considered to be nothing if not married to a man. I hope that these illustrated versions of her books will help you to question the past and the present, without ever forgetting to laugh ... and to dream!

SO, WHO WAS JANE AUSTEN?

Jane Austen was born in 1775 and had seven siblings. Her parents were well-respected in their local community, and her father was the clergyman for a nearby parish. She spent much of her life helping to run the family home, whilst reading and writing in her spare time.

Jane began to anonymously publish her work in her thirties and four of her novels were released during her lifetime: *Sense and Sensibility*, *Pride and Prejudice*, *Mansfield Park* and *Emma*. However, at the age of forty-one she became ill, eventually dying in 1817. Her two remaining novels, *Northanger Abbey* and *Persuasion*, were published after her death.

Austen's books are well-known for their comedy, wit and irony. Her observations about wealthy society, and especially the role women played in it, were unlike anything that had been published before. Her novels were not widely read or praised until years later, but they have gone on to leave a mark on the world for ever, inspiring countless poems, books, plays and films.

AND WHAT WAS IT LIKE IN 1817?

WAS IT A PEACEFUL ERA?

The British Navy was very important at the time Jane Austen was writing. The Napoleonic Wars (largely between Britain and France, to defend and expand their empires abroad) were just coming to an end, and the population generally held naval captains in high regard. The navy gave men without aristocratic titles an opportunity to rise up the ranks of society, but those such as Sir Walter Elliot could still look down their noses at these newly wealthy men, believing a distinguished family heritage was more important.

AT WHAT AGE DID PEOPLE GET MARRIED?

Women were generally expected to marry young – often in their teens. Wealthy women usually came out into society (meaning they were old enough to become engaged) between the ages of fifteen and nineteen and would find it harder to get a husband if they had not married by their early twenties. Women usually married men who were slightly older than themselves but could sometimes marry a man who was much older if it would provide them with financial security. Men were expected to begin to earn a living before they got married, in order to provide for their wife and their children. Wealthy families did not approve of young women falling in love with men who did not have money of their own – whether this was family money they had inherited, or money they earned from a successful career. Captain Frederick Wentworth would certainly have been more likely to have received Lady Russell's approval once he had earned his fortune at sea.

WERE ILLNESSES AND INJURIES MORE DANGEROUS?

There was no health service in the Regency period. People had to rely on local doctors who would have required payment for their skills, which meant that poor people often were not able to afford medical care. Medicines were much more limited – there were no tablets for pain relief and no antibiotics! This meant that it was much more dangerous when people got ill or had an accident. It would have been very scary when Anne's nephew fell down the stairs, but luckily his injuries weren't too serious. When Louisa had her accident at Lyme, her recovery period would have been much longer than in a modern hospital.

HOW DID PEOPLE SPEND THEIR FREE TIME?

The Georgians spent their free time in a variety of ways including playing card or board games, reading, dancing, drawing or going to the theatre. The type of concert which Anne and her family and friends attend in Bath would have been attended by wealthy society only, but lots of theatres would have had seats for both rich and poor. In big theatres in cities, the audience could become very rowdy, people would eat and drink through the performances, and sometimes they would even throw rotten vegetables on stage at acts they didn't like!

COLLECT THEM ALL!